# Textile Design Theory in the Making

# Textile Design Theory in the Making

Elaine Igoe

with contributions by Daniela Calabi, Elena Caratti,
Marianne Fairbanks, Tom Fisher, Marion Lean,
Mark Roxburgh and Rose Sinclair

BLOOMSBURY VISUAL ARTS
Bloomsbury Publishing Plc
50 Bedford Square, London, WC1B 3DP, UK
1385 Broadway, New York, NY 10018, USA
29 Earlsfort Terrace, Dublin 2, Ireland

BLOOMSBURY, BLOOMSBURY VISUAL ARTS and the Diana logo are trademarks
of Bloomsbury Publishing Plc

First published in Great Britain 2021
Paperback edition first published 2023

A catalogue record for this book is available from the British Library.

Library of Congress Cataloging-in-Publication Data
Names: Igoe, Elaine, editor.
Title: Textile design theory in the making / edited by Elaine Igoe.
Description: London ; New York : Bloomsbury Visual Arts, 2021. | Includescontributions
by Elena Caratti, Daniela Calabi, Marion Lean, RoseSinclair, Tom Fisher, Mark Roxburgh,
and Marianne Fairbanks. | Includesbibliographical references and index.
Identifiers: LCCN 2021001766 (print) | LCCN 2021001767 (ebook) |
ISBN9781350061569 (HB) | ISBN 9781350254107 (PB) | ISBN 9781350061576 (ePDF)|
ISBN 9781350061583 (eBook)
Subjects: LCSH: Textile design.
Classification: LCC NK8805 .T49 2021 (print) | LCC NK8805 (ebook) | DDC677/.022–dc23
LC record available at https://lccn.loc.gov/2021001766
LC ebook record available at https://lccn.loc.gov/2021001767

ISBN: HB: 978-1-3500-6156-9

# Contents

# Figures

# Contributors

**Daniela Calabi** is an architect, researcher and Associate Professor at the Department of Design at the Politecnico di Milano. Her research is focused on perception design and visual cultures, in particular, applied to the communication of landscapes and historical and contemporary identities. She also works on design education and basic design, addressing the theme of the translation of signs in texture design and types of texts. From 2005, Daniela Calabi has published numerous articles concerning research on texture design, in particular focusing on the concept of multimedia translation of formats and haptic and visual contents. In 2004 Calabi wrote the first edition of the book *Texture Design. Un percorso Basic*, with the introduction of Professor Attilio Marcolli and Professor Giovanni Baule. She has participated in international conferences promoting research concerning communication design applied to the identity of places through local texture design and craftwork, with experts in environmental design.

**Elena Caratti,** Architect, MA in e-design and PhD in design, is currently Associate Professor at the Design Department of Politecnico di Milano. Her research interests cover visual cultures and editorial design. She teaches visual cultures at the Design School of Politecnico di Milano and BA and MA courses in communication design. She also teaches research design critique at the PhD School in Design of Politecnico di Milano. In 2017 Caratti was co-editor with Giovanni Baule of the book *Design Is Translation. The Translation Paradigm for Design Culture* (the first edition of the book was published in Italian with Franco Angeli in 2016). It resonates with her contributory chapter reinforcing the concept for the reader and leading them to make comparisons with other fields of design (in this case communication design) while introducing new perspectives. Dr Elena Caratti is also an associate editor of *Studies in Material Thinking*, a peer-reviewed international online journal.

including the Museum of Art and Design, New York; the Smart Museum of Art, Chicago; and Copenhagen Contemporary, Denmark. Her work spans the fields of art, design and social practice, seeking to chart new material and conceptual territories, to innovate solution-based design and to foster fresh modes of cultural production.

**Tom Fisher** has been Professor in the School of Art and Design at Nottingham Trent University, UK, since 2007. He has led research funded by the AHRC and Defra, participating in work funded by WRAP. He is a member of the AHRC Peer Review College and reviews research bids for AHRC, ESRC and EPSRC. He is a member of the Design Research Society Council and lead the Special Interest Group OPEN (Objects, Practices, Experiences, Networks). He has led funded research on sustainable clothing (Defra) and industrial heritage (AHRC).

His background in craft practice (1985–94) has fed his work focused on embodied knowledge, the ethics of design and technologies, design, culture and innovation. He has led research on the textile heritage of Nottingham, particularly, as this relates to future innovation in an international context and has been the basis of his involvement in networks of researchers concerned with innovation. His recent work has included an AHRC-funded network that has focused on innovation in electronic textiles, and he is currently drawing on his work as a maker to develop work in the industrial heritage field on skill acquisition and transmission.

**Elaine Igoe** is Senior Lecturer in Textiles and Fashion at the University of Portsmouth, UK, and currently Visiting Tutor (Research) in the Department of Textiles at the Royal College of Art, London. Her research is concerned with theories of design as they relate to the creation of textiles, materials and surfaces. Igoe's doctoral study, written autoethnographically, was significant in developing new understandings of textiles within design research. She is a Review Board member for the Journal of Textile Design Research and Practice and for conferences internationally. Her recent articles and chapters focus on textiles in the post-digital era and the ethics of textile production methods.

**Marion Lean**'s doctoral design research at the Royal College of Art, UK, explores and object creation, physical, sensory experience and relationship building. Outcomes are working methods which contribute to the positioning of textile thinking as a means of knowledge production in design research. Previously, Marion worked in design, public engagement and communications roles in London having completed her masters in critical design from Goldsmiths in 2012 and textile design from Dundee in 2011.

**Mark Roxburgh** is Associate Professor of Design at the University of Newcastle, Australia. Mark's research interests cover design research, visual communication theory and practice, photographic theory and practice and user experience design. His PhD explored the central role that visual images and visual perception play in design, with a specific emphasis on how photographic images condition us to perceive, experience and transform the world in a self-replicating manner. His ongoing research pursuits have been developing a phenomenological theory of photography to counter the dominance of critical theory and semiotic deconstruction and developing a theory of design as a form of embodied perceptual synthesis to counter the dominance of the design problem-solving metaphor.

**Rose Sinclair** is a Design Lecturer (textiles) in the Design department at Goldsmiths, University of London, UK, where she teaches textiles- and design-related practice at postgraduate level. Her doctoral research focusses on Black British women and their crafting practices, and textiles, through the lens of textiles networks such as Dorcas Clubs and Dorcas Societies, through which she discusses migration, identity and settlement. Rose is also interested in the use of textiles networks as a form of participatory craft practice and public engagement in crafts. Rose continues to explore her textiles practice through participatory immersive workshops in localized pop-up shops, installations and presentations in museums and diverse spaces such as the V&A Museum London, the Bruce Castle Museum and House for An Art Lover. Rose has authored several textile books, her most recent being *Textiles and Fashion, Materials, Design and Technology* (2015). She is a member of the advisory board for Textile: Journal of Cloth and Culture and a member of the AHRC Stitching Together Research Network.

# Acknowledgements

The supervisory support and guidance I received during my doctoral studies at the Royal College of Art in the Department of Textiles were the foundation for the ideas developed in this book. I am so grateful to have had the opportunity to have been supervised by Dr Claire Pajaczkowska and Dr Prue Bramwell-Davies – both role models for me in my teaching and research. Likewise my fellow alumna, who remain friends and colleagues. I appreciate the encouragement to go on to publish my research as a book from Professor Jessica Hemmings and Victoria Mitchell back in 2013. More recently, conversations with colleagues and research students in the Department of Textiles at the Royal College of Art have also been key exploring the topics this book covers.

Notably, support and sabbatical funding from the Faculty of Creative and Cultural Industries at the University of Portsmouth has been vital in the development of this manuscript. I thank the fashion and textiles team in particular; helpful dialogue and practical support were given without question and were deeply valued. Thank you Susan Noble, Rachel Homewood, Christine Field and Lara Torres for friendship and unconditional collegiate support.

I acknowledge the contributions of the other authors of this book – not only for their work but also for their advice and patience. I reached out to these individuals to suggest a slightly different approach to academic bookmaking and I am glad to say that I found the right people. I recognize that they too have their own supporting structures to thank. In respect to this I specifically thank Anthony Burton on behalf of Marianne Fairbanks. New academic allegiances have been formed, and existing ones strengthened in the production of this book. In the course of making this book, other individuals have given of their time and energies and although the constraints of professional life meant the involvement had to end, your participation is appreciated. Thank you to the reviewers who give their time to undertake such activities of academic citizenship. I am grateful for the good guidance and support of Frances Arnold and her assistants at Bloomsbury Academic. Many thanks to the committee

My entire family has offered all types of support as I navigate what it is to be a first-generation academic and author. To my parents, my sisters and my brother, I feel your pride in me. Simon, Nara and Esmé, thank you for giving me joy and balance.

Elaine Igoe, January 2021

# Introduction

This book is a conversation about textile design and what it means to approach design from textility.

'Textility' is derived from a common etymological root of the Latin *texere*, meaning 'to weave', and the ancient Greek *techne*, meaning 'to make', and as such offers a model of making that is concerned with the 'slicing and binding of fibrous material' (Mitchell 1997: 7; Ingold 2010: 92). Mitchell goes on to highlight the further connection with 'text', offering textility as inference to a very particular way of making, speaking and writing, but also states: 'It is clear that textiles are not words and the differences between them benefit the conceptual apparatus of thought at the expense of its sensory equivalent' (Mitchell 1997: 8). Webster (1996: 99) explains theories of textuality and writerly texts via Roland Barthes's 'S/Z', in which he frequently uses textile and network metaphors to discuss the structure of texts and describes them as 'a surface over which the reader can range in any number of ways that the text permits'. The tension between the textuality of this publication and its relation to the concept of textility is consistent and apparent throughout this text. Negotiating the tension of this relationship, this *textasis* (see Chapter 15) has become my text-ile practice. I discovered this term 'textasis' in a 2009 essay from Maria Damon. She recounts her residency in Riga in 2008 for the E-text and Textiles Project. Damon's practice combined active poetics with textile practice and she produced small cross-stitched textile works that she sent to friends and colleagues, requesting their interaction and response on the pieces' textuality. One piece, 'B: Tiny Arkhive', was sent to Jewish-Canadian poet Adeena Karasick. BET or b is the second letter of the Hebrew alphabet and in this position is considered as female. Its numeric value is 2, which Karasick sees as signifying a doubling or a multiplicity. It represents a house, an archive – closed on three sides and open on one.

'You are an "Open House" which is at once in place, while deprived of any one

I read you as an embroidered network of socio-linguistic and hermeneutic relations.' (Damon 2009)

Karasick described the piece as 'an inscription of textasis'. This simple term is derived from the ancient Greek *tasis*, meaning stretching, tension or intensity. The example of this collaborative textile work connects ideas of gendering, the matrixial and relational, textuality and textility, representation, symbolism and the quantum, key concepts at various points in this book (Damon 2011).

Mitchell and Ingold's explication of the word 'textilic' should be held as one of the touchstones of this publication. I pick up from Ingold's 2010 paper *The Textility of Making* which outlines the marginalization of textilic approaches to design and making against the primacy of the architectonic model during the Enlightenment. To be textilic is to be textile like – a network, expansive, applicable. It sits between the architectonic and the hylomorphic as paradigms for thinking and making. I expand the notion of a textilic concept of knowledge-making into the matrixial (Ettinger 2005) which allows a feminist expansion of models of design and affords a connection between the exegesis of the design cognition and the designer (maker). The concept of the matrixial denotes trans-subjectivity in regard to the context, the designer(s), the process and the designed outcome.

I suggest that a matrixial approach sets up the connection between the designer and the outcomes and consequences their design spawn. The rhizomatic nature of the matrixial sets up the basis of an unending situation, only broken by external forces acting upon the scenario (see Chapter 13, *Making, Problems and Pleasures*).

Notions of textilic design and matrixial critiques and approaches to design here have been developed from an exploration into what textile design is at a fundamental level. However, my intention is to echo Anni Albers provocation at the start of her book *On Weaving* (1965: IX). *Textile Design Theory in the Making* is not only for those who identify with the disciplinary field of textile design but all those who find it difficult to associate with oversimplified, transactional or convergent models of design. Johan Redström's book *Making Design Theory* (2017) was one of the first to challenge these tenets and suggest that the development of design theory must recognize fluidity, complexity and indeed practice. On a less significant aspect, Redström (2017: 143) points to practice. The publication of this book is long preceded by Beverly Gordon's richly illustrated and veritable tome *Textiles: The Whole Story* (Gordon 2013). The image research to be found in Gordon's publication is extraordinary and, to date, unmatched. In many ways, this book cannot be read or fully understood without referring to it; certainly, it provides the best global and historical visualization of notions of how textility exists in the world.

In her preface, Gordon explains her discovery of the story of the Veil of *Maya* within Hindu philosophy (2013: 15). She points out that everything we think we know of our individualistic world is *Maya*. There exists a shimmering veil of Maya which has a purpose of shielding us from the essential wholeness of being but yet is there to remind us of the illusion of our incarnate existence, we are 'caught by its materiality'. Gordon presents her book as a textile installation which mimics the action of the veil of Maya.

I too got caught up in philosophical stories of mesh-like structures when conceptualizing my approach to bookmaking on textiles and the Buddhist philosophy of Indra's net struck me as significant.

> Far away in the heavenly abode of the great god Indra, there is a wonderful net which has been hung by some cunning artificer in such a manner that it stretches out infinitely in all directions. In accordance with the extravagant tastes of deities, the artificer has hung a single glittering jewel in each 'eye' of the net, and since the net itself is infinite in dimension, the jewels are infinite in number. There hang the jewels, glittering 'like' stars in the first magnitude, a wonderful sight to behold. If we now arbitrarily select one of these jewels for inspection and look closely at it, we will discover that in its polished surface there are reflected all the other jewels in the net, infinite in number. Not only that, but each of the jewels reflected in this one jewel is also reflecting all the other jewels, so that there is an infinite reflecting process occurring. (Cook 1973: 2)

Indra's net is an infinite mesh, matrix, grid, lattice, cat's cradle, weave, knit, cloth, fabric: but not only that, it is decorated and decorative, ornamental, glittery, bejewelled, draped so as to please the Gods. But the clever maker of this dazzling matrix remains unnamed. I have responded to the metaphor of Indra's net in both forming and representing the epistemology and methodology that evolved in the structure of this study. But rather than conceal the identity of the maker, through methods of autoethnography, the significance of my identity is not only the research process as they project and reflect onto and into one another in a recursive way. Each chapter is interstitial.

Chapter 1 *Too much to tell* outlines the feminist research approach that has shaped this book. The autoethnographic, narrative style used throughout is explained and the source of the guiding research questions is described. Adams and Holman Jones (2008: 379) outlining the dominant critique of autoethnographic research.

> . . . too much personal mess, too much theoretical jargon, too elitist, too sentimental, too removed, too difficult, too easy, too White, too Western, too colonialist, too indigenous. Too little artistry, too little theorizing, too little connection of the personal and political, too impractical, too little fieldwork, too few real-world applications.

This book's approach may be too much or too little for you. There may simply be too much or too little of its unapologetic narrative style. I intentionally use direct quotes heavily across the text, often suspended between paragraphs as an invitation for personal thought and interpretation before I offer my own. I aim to represent a multitude of voices rather than simply my own singular narration or interpretation. You will have already noted the purposeful use of personal pronouns. It is a monograph in many ways, but one in which I have invited discursive participation from scholars inside and outside of textiles. Their responses are included here alongside mine and collaboratively evidence 'the making' referred to in the title of this book.

Ramia Mazé talks of 'bookmaking as a feminist practice' (Mazé 2018). She describes her experience of being an author, editor and reviewer of several publications and says that

> my work reported here can be understood as a kind of 'practice-led' research, in which my reflections and conceptualizations have accumulated gradually on the basis of multiple experiences of bookmaking.

Mazé refers to and applies Jane Rendell's five modes of critical practice to her feminist bookmaking practice/practise (Rendell 2011 in Mazé 2018), namely collectivity, interiority, alterity, materiality and performativity. In *Textile Design Theory in the Making, collectivity* is manifested in the presentation of the book as a report on a methodology that is an actively and collectively developing one. *Interiority* supports philosophical approaches that explore connectedness

(Chapter 1) as well as the breadth of genres and ideologies it espouses and is played out in its structure, its *materiality*.

Chapter 3: *Talking textiles* is a short reflective text that encapsulates my research methods and tells a story – a truth about how interactions with the subject of my study – textile designers – played out and my agency within it as the researcher.

Chapter 4: *Design, thinking and textiles thinking* outlines research into the industrial structure of textile designing as well as pedagogic research in the field. This is contrasted with the development of design research and subsequently design thinking. Textile thinking as a concept is traced through the literature and 'textilic design' proposed as a development of such. After which begins a series of chapters whose content is extrapolated directly from conversations with textile designers and makers. Anonymous excerpts from these conversations are blended into polyphonic, non-linear texts called 'meshes' that intersperse the chapters.

Chapter 5: *Translating and transforming* investigates the role of the textile designer and textile as translator and semantic object, looking at design as an action of response, pledging back and gift- giving. It is paired with a chapter from Elena Caratti and Daniela Calabi on design as translation which is explored through notions of texture design.

Jessica Hemmings (2010) advocates the scholarly application of fiction, narrative and populist writings to develop an academic canon for textiles. Chapter 7: *A story of hard and soft: Modernism and textiles as design* takes a work of fiction by Paul Scheerbart entitled *The Gray Cloth* as a metaphor for the marginalization of textiles within modernist ideology and the subsequent impact on conceptions of textiles as design. The metaphoric comfortable emerald room (Scheerbart 2001) was for too long a space where textile designers quietened their expertise and subscribed to ideologies of craft and applied art.

This is further expanded in Chapter 8: *The gendered textile design discipline* which also draws on aspects of Chapter 5 to define how the discipline of textile design became gendered. In this chapter I expose a number of gendered metaphors for the entity of textiles, encompassing designers, designed outcomes, process and contexts. This is balanced by work from both Marion Lean and Rose Sinclair. In Chapter 9, Lean extends these ideas in the context of

In Chapter 11: *Paraphernalia and playing for design* I take on notions of playing in the process of designing, particularly with reference to playing cognitively as well as with materials at hand. The role of objects – stuff – for textile designers is the starting point for this chapter which picks back up notions of translation and taciturnity discussed earlier in the book. In Chapter 12, Tom Fisher provides us with a text in which he turns his attention to some objects he has made or found and their function in his career in 'making' with wood and in furniture design and design academia.

In Chapter 13: *Making, problems and pleasure* I return to earlier questions explored regarding design as problem-solving. I apply this to the field of textile design; mainstream textiles as well as innovation-led textile research. What 'problems' does textile design address itself to? Following this Mark Roxburgh develops an argument against the problematization of design. Through the work of Merleau-Ponty and Flusser and his own field of practice as an image-maker, Roxburgh critiques the prescriptive foundations of design theory and posits the perceptual basis of design as an alternative model for our understanding.

The concluding chapter, Chapter 15: *Elevated surfaces*, returns to relational conceptions of design and picks up the topics of the preceding chapters as it proposes definitions for what textile design is and how textilic design could be expanded. I have deliberately avoided approaches to concluding this book neatly; it is after all *in the making*. Instead the last pages provide an interruption of play, a breakage of the rhizome (Deleuze and Guattari 1980: 10), a point of inflection in the Deleuzian fold or a jewel in the (Indra's) net of textilic practice. In fact, this book closes not with my own words but an offshoot into the work of others – an epilogic account from Marianne Fairbanks, a textile practitioner across art, design and innovation. It is her work in fact that wraps this book, so, fittingly, she provides a co-emergent insight into how the thoughts drawn together in this chapter influence her textilic practice.

Writing this book has been an activity of looping, mending and reweaving. Repair as reparation to older ideas that myself and others have built upon. I naturally weave in work from others that has been created in the meantime or that now seems to have a place. My previous work has been cited by others and their work naturally critiques, builds, extends and applies those ideas. I wish to

This emerges from observations made through the contextualization of the textile design discipline within modernism, reappropriation and re-signification of textile metaphors, conversation, storytelling and restorying as analysis, often subsequently blended and meshed. You will notice that each of these research methods involves a dynamic: something is in something, something is in relation to something else, something combines with something else; notions of relationality, in inevitable partnership with tension, permeate the epistemology of this book at every level. This is attended to in the contextual discussion of design in regard to metamodernism in the concluding chapter, Chapter 15: *Elevated surfaces.*

My research methodology is a montage of qualitative methods, using autoethnography, storytelling and conversation to support textile designers in describing their own process and thinking. My aim is to situate these different stories in relation to the established context of design research. This volume aims to find a location between the types of fictional, poetic, social, cultural, political, historical writing found in textile culture publications and the current and broadest discourse of design theory. Daniela Rosner's book *Critical Fabulations: Reworking the Methods and Margins of Design* (2018) provides a significant influence on this publication. Rosner's work similarly uses narrative, first-person, feminist approaches to expose and 'rework' the margins of design. Key to her study is her exploration of textile structure and computation. Indeed a 'critical fabulation', as defined by Saidiya Hartman and later Rosner, is what I propose. This book aims to sit alongside *Critical Fabulations* in developing a body of alternative writings on what designing is.

I have invited contributions from authors whose research practice varies across forms of art, design and craft and who can offer additional viewpoints on the propositions of the key chapters. At the outset the editing relationship was set up as a dialogue. Their contributions are responses to my draft chapters and subsequently my final texts have been influenced by theirs. Their chapters have been minimally edited to retain style and voice and to respect authorship, avoiding any perceived hierarchy. The contributors include early to mid-career academics and distinguished professors. Three of the contributors I have never met but I sought out to find individuals who would be able to extend and probe my ideas in an interesting way. One is a long-standing and respected associate personal lives and global pandemics alongside the structural machinations of academic bookmaking prevented the realization of this initial proposal. Where this project has fallen short, I have engaged in citation politics (Mott and Cockayne 2017) referencing a majority of woman scholars. As mentioned earlier, Mazé and her collaborators' approach was not without obstacles set in place by the conventions of academia and publishing. This is my attempt to develop an additional example of how bookmaking can be a form of feminist design practice.

As you read, you will note marked differences in the style of writing and research approach throughout. This is intentional and communicates a very real shift that I experienced from an objective research style to one where my subjectivity became vital to the research. This shift occurred in response to several contingent factors in both the personal and academic realms of my lived experience.

> The individual is both site and subject of these discursive struggles for identity and for remaking memory. Because individuals are subject to multiple and competing discourses in many realms, their subjectivity is shifting and contradictory, not stable, fixed, rigid. (Richardson 2000: 929)

I wanted to make my own discursive struggle evident across these pages, to use mine and others' writing, as Richardson suggests, as a method (and as such, record) of qualitative inquiry.

When I learnt printed textile design, ensuring that you trim your sample so that it appears as if it is cut from a roll of fabric with no borders was one of the first presentation conventions we encountered. In terminology borrowed from graphic design or photography this would be called a 'full-bleed' method of presentation. My textile practice bleeds into and reflects onto the written and visual work of others, some of which have been directly referenced and some not; some give their names and contributions here, others not. All are respectfully acknowledged as essential to this polyphony.

> There is no longer a tripartite division between a field of reality (the world) and a field of representation (the book) and a field of subjectivity (the author). Rather, an assemblage establishes connections between certain multiplicities drawn from each of these orders, so that a book has no sequel nor the world as its object nor one or several authors as its subject. (Deleuze and Guattari 1980/2008: 25)

# 1

# Too much to tell

## Autoethnography

Developed over the past fifty years as a response to colonialism and issues of representation, autoethnography is used as a critical approach to knowledge-making across a range of fields. Carolyn Ellis, a leading autoethnographer, tells how she came to develop her autoethnography as a poststructuralist, postmodern, feminist researcher contesting issues of authority, representation, voice and method (Adams, Holman Jones and Ellis 2015: 3). She describes how, as an approach to her field of ethnography, it united her 'sociological eye with a communicative heart'. Autoethnography was a way to overcome the crisis of representation, to avoid generalizing and homogenous positivism and to recognize the subjectivity of the situated researcher.

> Autoethnography is a qualitative method – it offers nuanced, complex, and specific knowledge about particular lives, experiences, and relationships rather than general information about large groups of people. (Adams, Holman Jones and Ellis 2015: 21)

The research presented in this book began as personal questions, doubts and stories I told myself, about myself and my situation. I came to a point in my career in design academia where these feelings and thoughts surfaced in direct confrontation to what I was rationally, objectively researching. It got to a point where I was forced to deal with them. Autoethnography permitted me to take the route that allowed for complexity and subjectivity, recognizing this juncture as a 'personal-cultural entanglement' (Adams, Holman Jones and Ellis 2015: 22).

3. Demonstrate the power, craft and responsibilities of stories and storytelling
4. Take a relationally responsible approach to research practice and representation

This book seeks to contribute to design research and develop design theory. It does this through valuing collective subjective experience in the field of textile design, expressed through narrative methods, both directly told and restoried or fabulated. It is structured through and upon a framework of critical relationality – informing both its premise and its delivery.

Ellis and Bochner's paper *Autoethnography, Personal Narrative, Reflexivity: Researcher as Subject* (2000) tells us a story about what it is to be an autoethnographer, what it is to learn about autoethnography and how the approach developed within the broader field of narrative enquiry. Its storied style makes it easy to read and accessible, even though its content is complex. Reading Ellis and Bochner's work inspired me to write large the changes that have happened throughout my research journey, accepting that edges of my various bits of writing are ragged and frayed, not smooth and sharp. They overlay, enmesh and entangle; they don't tessellate. And I won't try to make them, either.

> [T]he researcher's personal experience becomes important primarily in how it illuminates the culture under study. Reflexive ethnographies range along a continuum from starting research from one's own experience to ethnographies where the researcher's experience is actually studied alongside with other participants, to confessional tales where the researcher's experience of doing the study becomes the focus of investigation. (Ellis and Bochner 2000)

Through reflective writing, through co-creating stories with other textile designers, through the structuring and presentation of this book, I am expressing an autoethnography. I am expressing my life, my character, my constraints, my relationships and my position on textile design in the world. In this book can be seen the evidence of the story of its development. In some ways I wish I could be braver, dating each piece of writing, placing it firmly at the point at which it was thought, written and rewritten, resisting polishing and tessellation. I do consider this text as my creative research practice. My textile design aesthetic

# Conversation

The key tool I have used to retrieve the fragments of experience is the recorded conversation. The key thoughts presented in this book were based on a series of fifteen recorded conversations which took place between February 2009 and March 2011 and developed through countless informal conversations, emails and further academic work in the years since. These recorded conversations were initially set up as unstructured/semi-structured interviews, but most played out as conversations. At the time, I berated myself as researcher for jumping in and talking, but it was too difficult not to. I was talking to textile designers. I am a textile designer. I teach textile designers. Most of the so-called 'interviews' had been arranged through mutual contacts, or we were fellow alumni. I was inextricably connected to the people I was talking with. I felt at ease and let myself seep into the talking. The individuals I spoke to were students of textile design, world-famous textile designers, textile studio owners, designer makers, textile innovators, commercial textile designers, textile design lecturers, embroidery designers, print designers and weave designers. Some I was in awe to be speaking to, others were literally old friends. They took place in my research space, in cafes, in their studios; I spoke to friends over the phone while they were at work and strangers invited me into their kitchens to talk over homemade soup. Each scenario was interpersonal: trans-subjective encounters, to use Ettinger's terminology.

For the first set of conversations in 2009, I arrived with a list of specific questions that I hoped to pop when the moment should arise. They covered these main areas: working and thinking methods for textile design, communicating design ideas and outcomes for textiles, self-awareness and identification with the concept of textile design. This list of questions often stifled the conversation as it began to emerge. The talk would then begin to loosen and I would steer it ridiculously back to my questions, the dialogue jumping about wildly.

One particular question proved problematic: why do we design textiles? The designers found this question difficult, both to understand and to answer. This question later morphed into me asking about the 'role of textile design'. I wanted to know how the textile designers see the significance of their work.

For the ensuing conversations from 2010 and 2011, I allowed a more natural

My personality, my relationships, my research expertise (or lack of it) and my textile knowledge were all brought to bear on each conversation. This is evident as the textile designers talked to me about tutors we had had in common, shortened names for our alma mater and initialisms for certain trade events. In *Living Narrative*, Elinor Ochs and Lisa Capps champion the conversation, specifically personal narratives and everyday storytelling, as a means of exploring narrative for three key reasons. It affords an inherent open-endedness, is a medium for airing unresolved events and it elicits familiarity (2001: 6). They describe how conversational narratives reveal the vernacular and a way of ordering, explaining and establishing a position on experience (2001: 57).

Some of the mutual connections we held were unknown at the outset, only coming to light precisely through conversation, in turn simultaneously building and altering the nuance of the talk. The familiarity that was often established at times turned the direction of the conversation back to myself, the textile designers asking me about my design work and research. Other times, I do this for myself, offering up thoughts and comments for debate that are unique to that specific conversation. This dialogue meant that although I was always the initiator of the talk, I did not hold all the control over it. It became a conversation rather than interview because of its dialogical content. The active participation from both parties changed and altered the direction and content of the talk (Ochs and Capps 2001: 55).

Informal conversations and encounters have naturally influenced my approach to bookmaking. It so often goes without saying but it shouldn't. Conference presentations and invitations to speak at events that seemed to me at first to be a tangent opened up new areas and connections – new words too. Academics finding my (old) work for the first time allowed me to see its currency as well as its flaws. Students using, testing and challenging my work to make their own new work is so directly encouraging and invigorating. Being part of that process as a PhD supervisor is a privilege as well as a prompt as a researcher.

## Stories and fabulations

The outcomes of these conversations can be read as narratives, or 'everyday others show new ideas and perspectives surfacing within that moment. The notion of extracting rational 'truth' from these stories is nonsensical. Each textile designer has told me a story about their experience of being a textile designer. Walter Benjamin parallels everyday storytelling with the physicality and materiality of making.

> [A story] does not aim to convey the pure essence of the thing, like information or a report. It sinks the thing into the life of the storyteller, in order to bring it out of him again. Thus, traces of the storyteller cling to the story the way the handprints of the potter cling to the clay vessel. (Benjamin 1936: 91)

And the structure and content of the stories told to me at that time were affected by me: my own story and my own questions.

> For it is granted to him to reach back to a whole lifetime (a life, incidentally, that comprises not only his own experience but no little of the experience of others; what the storyteller knows from hearsay is added to his own.) His gift is the ability to relate his life; his distinction, to be able to tell his entire life. (Benjamin 1936: 108)

These stories do not hold truths but commonalities of experience that might develop new knowledge and understanding, 'openly or covertly, something useful'(1936: 86):

In fact, one can go on and ask oneself whether the relationship of the storyteller to his material, human life, is not in itself a craftsman's relationship, whether it is not his very task to fashion the raw material of experience, his own and that of others, in a solid, useful and unique way. (Benjamin 1936: 107)

The *Talking Textiles* chapter offers a piece of creative writing for which I used a process recommended by Ellis and Bochner (2000: 752). They suggest using a process of emotional recall where the writer revisits a scene emotionally and physically. In this piece, I blended two conversation scenarios together to help indicate the trans-subjective encounter that took place, focusing on motifs of interconnectedness and reflexivity. Ellis and Bochner highlight the advantage of recalling these emotions as close to the experience as possible; however, for me, it was what I experienced in the years between that allowed me to reflect and connect the two scenarios, offering a perspective on my research methodology and methods.

fiction as factually accurate, polyphonic and scenical, and centrally positions the researcher/author as character. The various pieces of creative non-fiction that punctuate this book were written at different times: they are independent but are connected through my experience as textile designer and researcher.

Ronald Pelias (2011: 660) describes how writing might function as a both a realization and record. He cites M. L. Rosenthal's quote from 1987 suggesting that writing is 'the unfolding of a realization, the satisfying of a need to bring to the surface the inner realities of the psyche', and remarks on the difference of 'writing up' and 'writing into'. I use words to help me discover what I want to say. Pelias goes on to explain how realizations recorded and brought about through writing can be felt with confidence or some level of doubt, but that these realizations importantly 'unfold on a continuum from the personal to the public', supporting feminist ideology; he then quickly cautions on separating the personal and the public/political. The writing that makes up this book moves between and conjoins both objective and subjective writing styles as required, recognizing that both have their place and that all writing is a record. Older pieces of work have been cut and spliced with very recent writing and reconfigured. Personal narratives sit alongside conventional styles; mythologies and literature are incorporated into analytical texts; the sections do not flow directly into one another but largely rely on the heuristics of the reader to establish the connections.

In *Critical Fabulations* (2018) Daniela Rosner uses 'fabulation' to displace established understandings of design. To fabulate is to talk or narrate in fables – to invent, concoct and fabricate. Rosner takes this concept from writer Saidiya Hartman who developed critical fabulation in her own work as an approach to re-storying. Rosner describes how in her fabulated account of a project which combined quilting and electrical engineering in a design context, she hopes to expand the opportunities for the groups and spaces in which design takes place and in doing so 'reorient what lies ahead' (Rosner 2018: 1). Rosner clearly sets out her feminist technoscience research approach and based on this challenges established design theory. She designates these as four dimensions:

- Individualism – design as an aggregation of individuals.
- Objectivism – design as science paradigm promotes rationality and

Avoiding setting up a binary position, Rosner describes the tactics (Rosner 2018: 15) with which she challenges these dimensions:

- Alliances – demands that design recognizes that it operates in concert with and not on behalf of the groups for whom it works.
- Recuperations – 'the possibility of design to ignite recuperations enlivening neglected histories of encounter' (Rosner 2018: 14).
- Interferences – propose alternative frames of analysis to expand and change existing regimes.
- Extensions – design is remade over time, across contexts and in circulations of practice.

There are two stories or fabulations I wish to tell about this research journey. Both are true.

The first might be considered a tragedy (Booker 2004). The protagonist (myself) embarks on a quest, only to find that the quest takes her into unpredictable territories, ones she is unfamiliar with and unprepared for. She finds that the decisions she makes are naïve and ungrounded and she realizes that she cannot go back. Only the guidance of her elders can lead her back to safety.

The second, a tale of rebirth (Booker 2004). Our main character is captivated by a dream of a new reality and works doggedly to achieve the status she so desires. The voices and actions of others reinforce her fascination. Only those who know her best realize that she is looking in the wrong places to fulfil her dreams. The story builds to a crescendo that results in a moment of clarity for the protagonist, who comes to recognize that she already possesses the knowledge and material required to manifest a new reality of greater worth and meaning than she could have ever dreamt of.

The ontological paradigm or 'world view' of this study can be considered to oscillate between the constructivist and participatory/postmodern, as outlined by Lincoln, Lynham and Guba (2011: 102), and its connected epistemology is well illustrated by Ettinger's matrixial, intersubjective encounter. Holding this 'world view' means that for me, of the two tales, I must select the second as my plot. It's a story that emphasizes the socially constructed nature of knowledge, and also that:

The 'multiple mental constructions' that I show here are stories of what it is to design textiles: my own story and those of others. The aim of gathering and thinking around these stories is to prompt a deeper understanding and articulation of the knowledge and thinking crucial to textile design in others and myself.

I intend that the stories, gathered in different ways and at different times over fifteen years and hermeneutically told through my own research practice, should create a layered polyphony, not one singular, uniform voice.

## Enmeshing

As an analysis method I have elected to 're-story' the stories (Craig and Huber 2007) I have co-created. Using transcripts from recorded conversations and notes and memories from other encounters, I have developed a number of montaged texts that interweave our subjective experiences and understandings of textile design. The resultant 'meshes', as I have called them, resemble a 'fusion of horizons' (Gadamer 1960: 306) that offer perspectives on textile design.

Ochs and Capps (2001:6) discuss the 'polyphonic and indeterminate quality of human events and non-events' as captured by writers such as Dostoevsky and Tolstoy: although they can be hard to describe in the way that they oscillate between often conflicting perspectives in a non-linear fashion, they better resemble human experience. They encourage an understanding of narrative as 'fuzzy' and as a means for imagining possibilities, shifting mindsets and for acting from a place of uncertainty.

The way I have written the 'meshes' intentionally retains the idiosyncrasies of the speech patterns and vocabulary of the participants but are intersected and interwoven to emphasize specific commonalities and themes that arose. The effect is polyphonic: it is clear that the texts did not originate from only one individual, but it is still difficult to identify individual voices and narratives.

They are called meshes in order to highlight this interwoven character and for the metaphor it affords. Meshes filter and refine. These texts have been created to enable me to sift through the discussions and extract key concepts. Creating the meshes required iterative close reading and recall activities. As I did so, I noted down keywords and concepts that arose from each one, creating extractions of reconsider the groupings of commonalities. Some phrases are reused in several of the meshes as the complexity of meaning in certain sentences became more and more apparent with each rereading. I noted that I was developing different ways of understanding these stories, these truths.

The meshes are devised as a means of defining important characteristics of textile design. They are of course innately connected through myself and the other textile designers whose stories they are founded on. I like to consider the meshes as transparent, pliable 'supple fabrications' (Mitchell 1997), woven together (Bateson 2000) and layered up in their retelling of the narrative of textile design, piling up to become something more substantive, as described by Walter Benjamin in *The Storyteller* (1936: 92):

'That slow piling one on top of the other of thin, transparent layers which constitutes the most appropriate picture of the way in which the perfect narrative is revealed through the layers of a variety of retellings.'

Four meshes are interspersed throughout the book and they align with the main chapters retaining the spoken, conversational quality of the words. As well as the four meshes that punctuate the book I also include pieces of reflective and creative writing, both from myself and some of the contributing authors. These texts invite further interpretations, beyond those I have involved myself with at this stage.

The significance and importance of re-evaluating research is discussed by Margery Wolf in *A Thrice Told Tale*, in which she publishes three depictions of an event that took place while she was conducting anthropological field research in Taiwan in 1960. They include a piece of fiction, field notes and records of conversations and observations and an academic paper, some written at the time, others more recently: all written by her. She also provides a brief rationalized summary and commentary on each depiction. Wolf adopts a feminist critique of ethnography and asserts that the retelling of the original story in different styles to different audiences yielded different outcomes and conclusions. Wolf recognizes the requirement to be reflexive – questioning methodology and process. She states how important it was to return to her field notes when re-evaluating the fictional piece she wrote, and yet these only provide a summary, 'a partial and incomplete version of reality' (Wolf 1992: 87). They are in themselves un-self-conscious fictions.

In the preparation of this book, the meshes have been reworked again – an activity akin to securing, reinforcing, mending and repair or as Rosner might say an act of recuperation. This activity brings conversations and thoughts from the past back into focus; recognizing a lineage over time. As soon as I put these re-stories, these fabulations into words they become too fixed of course. The process of developing a publication offers critical review but the outcome is fixed in time – the time of reading often being a good while after thinking or writing. But I present them as meshes; they are a flexible tool, a substrate or a mediating material for further researchers.

## Metaphor

Our ordinary conceptual system, in terms of which we both think and act, is fundamentally metaphorical in nature. The concepts that govern our thought are not just matters of the intellect. They also govern our everyday functioning, down to the most mundane details. Our concepts structure what we perceive, how we get around in the world and how we relate to other people. Our conceptual system thus plays a central role in defining our everyday realities. If we are right in suggesting that our conceptual system is largely metaphorical, then the way we think, what we experience and what we do every day is very much a matter of metaphor (Lakoff and Johnson 1980/2003: 3).

Lakoff and Johnson's classic text describes the unavoidable significance of metaphor to thinking, knowing and being: as their title points out, we 'live by' metaphors. And indeed they are fundamental to this book: abundant in the texts I have read and responded to; latent in my conversations with supervisors and textile designers; and essential to my thinking, writing and analytical processes. Andrew Ortony's revised compilation *Metaphor and Thought* (1993) provides key texts on the significance of metaphor, not only within language but also cognition. The very premise for the epistemological foundation of what I propose is set; relationality is represented by the metaphorical and feminist content of the concept of the matrixial (Ettinger 2006a). Laurel Richardson describes feminist researchers' introduction of the 'theory is story' metaphor, recognizing the importance of narrating their lived experience and how these is crucial to how people account for their personal world view, how they make sense of reality, how they set and solve problems and how they think. He asserts that metaphor can be considered as simultaneously a product (like a frame) as well as a generative process. Schön alludes to the fact that what is viewed, framed or set through a metaphor (in his example, the problematics of social policy) are also processed by it, generating new perspectives. This notion of 'framing' allows the influence of viewpoints and subjectivity on a problematic situation. Schön recognizes how storytelling invites varying viewpoints, shaping, setting or framing a problem, using metaphors as interpretive devices that invite critical analysis.

> In short, we can spell out the metaphor, elaborate the assumptions which flow from it, and examine their appropriateness in the present situation. (Schön 1978: 138)

Schön goes on to emphasize his use of the term 'problem setting' over 'problem solving' believing that the way in which an objective is framed is more important than selecting specific methods to achieve them. He says that stories have 'problem-setting potency' (Schön 1978: 150) which is sometimes derived from their underlying generative metaphor. Schön's comments set up the connection between metaphor and narrative that has become so pervasive in my research. The development and exploration of the 'textile design as female entity' involves the interaction of 'entailments' and 'reverberations' (Lakoff and Johnson 1980/2003: 140), not least the paradigm of 'design as feminine'. These entailments and reverberations act to specify the metaphor and how it may be used and understood. Metaphors can have wildly different meanings for different people based on their culture and lived experience. If we do 'live by' metaphor, I must explore the assumptions held within the generative metaphor I use here, while challenging those embodied within the established understanding of design theory and the metaphors involved.

Returning to Schön's terminology of framing, this sets up an example of 'frame awareness, frame conflict and frame restructuring' (Schön 1978: 150). In this research, the frame of understanding textile design is identified, challenged and reformed to allow a feminist critique of design theory through textile.

## 2

# Matrixial meaning

### Kyoto, Japan, 2010

Its architect, Hiroshi Hara, called it *The Matrix*. The complex curving network of steel beams of the roof of Kyoto Railway Station is evident from the main concourse. You only achieve the real sense of it when emerging up through the vast building on its seemingly endless escalators that transport you past floors and floors of retail outlets, restaurants and hotels and platforms.

The heat of the August afternoon was getting to me. My husband was off elsewhere. It was just too hot for me. The architecture of the place, although dated, was compelling. I reached the humid air of the open rooftop and stopped to take in the view of the Kyoto skyline, familiar as a metropolis but hemmed in by mountainous hills on all sides.

At that point I had already been considering the notion of nets and meshes metaphorically in relation to textiles, and the term 'matrix' struck a chord with this way of thinking. The information plaques dotted around the roof garden explained the etymological basis of the word as 'womb' or a 'place or medium where something is developed'. The building's roof forms a literal matrix in its mesh-like qualities and is womb-like in the sense that it does not entirely enclose the building. It creates a space that is at once open and closed, allowing the architectural experience to change and alter in respect to the interplay of natural and artificial light, the weather and inside/outside occurrences.

On returning home, I wanted to express the matrix-like nature of textiles in my writing, clumsily using 'matrixical' (a non-existent word of my own creation); however, some internet searching soon unearthed for me the term 'matrixial' theoretical discourse. Ettinger's texts are linguistically creative and challenging. With no experience in psychoanalytical texts I had to persevere but eventually an understanding began to emerge that revealed fruitful resonances.

Griselda Pollock and Judith Butler provide many critical explorations of Ettinger's written and artistic works. Pollock, in her article 'Mother trouble: the maternal-feminine in phallic and feminist theory in relation to Bracha Ettinger's elaboration of matrixial ethics' (2009) begins with an excerpt from Sylvia Plath's poem 'Love Letter', written in 1960, six months after the birth of her daughter. Pollock draws our attention to its opening line: 'Not easy to state the change you made.' She suggests that the poem is a commentary on both prenatal and postnatal maternity and an exemplar of the trans-subjectivity and co-emergence that Ettinger advocates in her theory:

> I took the intrauterine meeting as a model for human situations and processes in which non-I is not an intruder, but a partner in difference. The Matrix reflects multiple and/or partial joint strata of subjectivity whose elements recognize each other without knowing each other. (Ettinger (1993) cited in Pollock (2009: 5))

Pollock explains how Ettinger chooses to use the word 'matrix' for its literal Latin definition of 'womb' but distinctly for its definition as a complex, generating structure. Just a few weeks after our visit to Japan, I learned that I was pregnant. The coincidence of happening upon matrixial theory during my very early and as yet unknown pregnancy of course meant that I had a certain filter through which to read Ettinger's theories that helped me to understand more deeply her use of the term.

Ettinger (2006b: 219) is clear in her use of this term linked to its 'originary' mode that emerges neither as biologically nor socially gendered. She conceives of a womb/matrix as the site of human potentiality for difference-in-co-emergence and emphasizes the matrixial psychic space as concerned with severality and shareability over collectivity, community or organized-ness. Ettinger clearly states how the matrixial is not an alternative to phallic-centric theoretical models but resides and exists beyond/alongside it. It avoids setting up in opposition to the masculine or dichotomies of feminine and masculine. This very notion challenges several aspects of established psychoanalytical theory. Pollock explains that it co-existing with but shifting the phallic, in which the subject is fragile, susceptible and compassionate to the unknown other who is, nonetheless, a partner in the situation but a partner-in-difference. (Pollock 2009: 5)

Subjectivity may be, also and at the same time, for different ends and effects, encounter. (Pollock 2009: 14)

Matrixial theory supports a research approach that promotes the inclusivity of the researcher in the research project and would deny the notion that the two could be separated. In my own experience, it is undeniable that I am in a trans-subjective 'encounter' with my research. I see how my life has shaped the developments of my learning, thinking, making, teaching and writing in both explicit and implicit terms.

## Portsmouth, UK, 2012

And now as I return to work after my maternity leave, the necessary completion of this project impacts on the choices my family has made in the organization of our lives to help me achieve my goals.

I have been enrolled as a research student for seven years, and during this time I have (at the very least!) travelled, taught and been taught, got married, been pregnant, given birth and become a working parent. This very piece of writing, in its content, form and how and when it was written, has been inescapably affected by all those factors, plus many more. I have always found it very difficult to find a title for my research project: of course it is tricky to capture the essence of an extended piece of writing in one or two sentences, but when viewed as a developing entity in itself in the way that matrixial theory proposes, how can it be named before it exists in its own right? Its subjectivity is 'fragile and susceptible'. Educational establishments and research councils require clear proposals, outlines, milestones and projected costings when embarking on a research project, but these schemata can never be anything more than fictions. This approach supports a binary approach to thinking with the researcher cloven of involvement in it. Taking the notion of co-emergence and the trans-subjective matrixial encounter further and exploring it in the context of the trimesters of pregnancy, my pregnancy, helps me to make sense creativity, femininity and the maternal and those of Julia Kristeva and Luce Irigaray:

> Thus, Ettinger opens up a new field that radically introduces the concept of the pre-natal/pre-maternal situation of primordial encounter as a basis for recognising another dimension of subjectivity, fantasy and thought that is not all about organs. It concerns structures, logics and affects, as well as garnered or remembered sensations, retroactively (nachträglich) caught up as the basis for both thinking ethics (relations to the other) and aesthetics (transmitted affects and transformations of/in/between the other(s). (Pollock 2009: 7)

I emphasize specific words in this quotation from Pollock as it so clearly outlines how useful the theory of the matrixial is for understanding textiles. Textiles, as designed, made objects (of material culture) are all about structure, logic (/function) and so richly concerned with affect, aesthetics, sensation, communication and relationality. What then can be said about the design (and making) process through the framework of the matrixial? How can Ettinger's textile metaphors be mirrored back to help us understand textile design? Ettinger continues where so many others have started by using textile terms as metaphors in her theories. She describes vibrating 'strings', 'threads' and 'weaving' to describe her version of co-poeisis.

> She is weaving and being woven. She bears witness in the woven textile and texture of psychic transsubjectivity. (Ettinger 2006: 196)
>
> Each psyche is a continuity of the psyche of the other in the matrixial borderspace. We thus metabolize mental imprints and traces for one another in each matrixial web whose psychic grains, virtual and affective strings and unconscious threads participate in other matrixial webs and transform them by borderlinking in metramorphosis. (Ettinger 2005: 704–5)

She describes 'metramorphosis' as 'a process of interpsychic communication and transformation that transgresses the borders of the individual subject and takes place between several entities' (Ettinger 2004: 77). 'Through this process the limits, borderlines, and thresholds conceived are continually transgressed or dissolved, thus allowing the creation of new ones' (Ettinger (1992) cited in Pollock (2009: 3)).

Thus, the matrixial sits as the epistemological framework for this study,

## A New Place, 2019

Oh how true this feels. Coming back to this means a remembering – sometimes difficult, sometimes not. This thing lives now. It has made a connection to others. It exists. But now I return to it and it must take a new shape. It needs it. Things have changed. No. Things are the same, but I didn't know it then. It is both then, now and the future. This process is asymmetrical but is temporal and has flex, like the stretching and changing of shadows over the course of a day. I move around this thing with a different viewpoint, different aspects are extended and more dense. Occasionally I see the traces of a secondary shadow depending on the angle I see it from. I am putting it back out there in a different form now. The rhizome was forced to branch then but now again, it must too.

> This multiple diachronous as well as synchronous transitivity is asymmetrical, regressive, remembering and at the same time, anticipatory and projective into living futures to come. (Pollock 2009: 9)

Pollock's statement summarizes the generative aspect of the matrixial theory, the severality that Ettinger emphasizes. This facet is crucial in my application of the matrixial as a framework for both my research approach.

This act of returning described earlier in 'A New Place' also cites Ettinger's series of artworks entitled *Eurydice*, where her 'disrupted' photocopies are then painted into in an attempt to capture what was lost in the process of making (metramorphosis). In the attempted 'mending' of the image, it is altered further, resulting in a multilayered image.

> If one is to see Eurydice . . . . One must find the history of what she cannot narrate, the history of her muteness, if one is to recognise her. This is not to supply the key, to fill the gap, to fill in the story, but to find the relevant remnants that form the broken landscape that she is. (Butler 2006: xi)

In the parable of Orpheus and Eurydice, Orpheus's plaintive music provides him with an opportunity to rescue his dead wife from the underworld with the caution that he should lead the way and not look at her until they have reached the light. However, once Orpheus steps foot into the light, he is tempted and he glances around to see her. At once Eurydice sinks back to the underworld and is gone. Ettinger's Eurydice series, the parable itself and Butler's description above

Actions of shedding, disruption, reworking, mending, alteration, layering and collaboration all set in its temporal contexts are important. Using Denzin and Lincoln's metaphor of pentimento extends these ideas.

Definitions of pentimento not only cover the act of 'painting out' certain aspects in an artwork and the subsequent traces of those original marks and their alterations but also describe these marks once they have been revealed. It describes emergence represented simultaneously through layering and revelation. It implicates the involvement of different individuals and their subjectivity over time, in making marks, adapting them, reading/viewing them and revealing them. Those marks, dismissed and erased, once revealed can shed new light on a subject, telling new stories, inviting alternative understandings of knowledge and meaning. Pentimento also covers the description of an act of remorse and repentance, and in this delivers an accompanying narrative that begs exploration.

The pentimento of this book is the hypothesis of alternative understandings of design. The feminization of textile design as process and object has contributed to its invisibility in the pages of design research, allowing a hegemony to develop within the academic design research community. Like Judith Butler's summary of the parable of Eurydice, I am not filling in gaps in a story but developing one by uncovering existing traces, on top of which I can find correspondence with experiences of textile design. Through this act of layering, a new narrative emerges.

# 3

## Talking textiles

### A story

I've made sure that I look right, wearing something colourful – hair big and frizzy. I knock at the door of the terraced townhouse. After some time, a woman in her late forties answers the door with a welcoming smile and I recognize her. Her sweet, bright, flat shoes and patterned tights make me like her instantly. She's wearing a vivid turquoise angora cardigan, so fluffy that it is difficult to make out her silhouette. Visually, her top half appears to diffuse into her surroundings. She invites me into the house and we go into the kitchen. Oh the kitchen! – a view onto the garden, a repainted dresser proudly displaying dozens of apothecary jars and other glass vases each holding some or other lovely flower. Her black crinkled skirt is full and reaches just below her knee. It moves and sways merrily as she walks. A beautiful short-haired grey cat slopes in through the door as she offers me a hot drink and weaves itself through her legs to its bowl. Fresh ginger tea? (Just what I need with this cold) Mug in hand I follow her down the narrow staircase, past bolts of fabrics semi-wrapped in ripped brown paper, to the studio basement. There is music playing, a radio station. The studio is so full of stuff that I don't know where to look first. I am aware that I need to take in every detail, record it somehow in my head or on paper . . . somehow? Let me try and recall it now. The décor is pretty crumby in comparison to upstairs; it's definitely a workshop. There are threads, beads and dust collecting in the corners of the skirting board. The lighting is difficult on this grey day, difficult anyway in a basement I imagine. In the far corner there are floor-to-ceiling bookshelves, filled with large, heavy books on to describe them – 'objects' might be too grand a term to use to describe this collection of a dusty taxidermy monkey, samples of some kind of flooring, faded silk flowers, a bundle of old ladies headscarves, a cheap beaded coin purse emblazoned with 'Las Vegas', bones, fir cones and countless other such random paraphernalia. Paraphernalia seems much more appropriate a word to use, its meaning evolved from the phrase 'paraphernalia bona' ('paraphernal goods') from the Latin *parapherna*, 'a woman's property besides her dowry', articles of personal property, especially clothing and ornaments, which did not automatically transfer from the property of the wife to the husband by virtue of the marriage. Paraphernalia of course also means the pieces of equipment or products associated with or necessary for an activity. These items, collected by her, I know only too well are absolutely necessary to the process of designing textiles. They are about colour, texture, humour, memories, material, surface qualities, symbolism, culture and personality.

She's already coming out with great stuff that I should be recording! I'm trying to take it all in while responding to her comments. I shall just have to try and write it all down on the Tube later. As she shows me around the studio, she briefly introduces me to the three or four young women who are working hunched over tables, laptops and ironing boards, whom I have just noticed behind all the stuff. I'm unsure as to who actually works there and which ones are on work placements. She asks me where I studied. Loughborough, I said. Oh she said, Lucy went there didn't you Lucy. Lucy and I did not know one other; she was clearly much younger than me, but we gave each other a gentle smile, enough to recognize some level of sorority that seemed to please the woman I'd come to speak to about textile design. I sip my ginger tea as I walk. She begins to point out pieces of work that were framed and/or hung on the wall. She tells me that pieces like that used to be sold as designs for textiles. They were collages, craft pieces, textile doodlings, paintings onto wood. They were so far from what Lucy and the others were working on – digital designs, sublimation prints, screenprints and embroideries, scaled-down garment fronts. The studio 'tour' is soon complete and we take a seat at her desk or 'area', as there isn't really a desk to speak of, more a 'clearing' in the undergrowth of 'paraphernalia'. The conversation flows seamlessly as she asks me what I want to know. (I want to know that I'm right and not imagining all this, emperor's new clothes style – of course I don't say this, I formal within seconds. I wish I'd had the recorder on from the moment she opened the front door. But I'm not supposed to do that, am I, that's not what good researchers do. We diligently work through my questions. I try not to talk too much myself, sipping my now cool ginger tea, leaning away so as not to record my slurps. Just remembered, I should be taking notes, I start to scrawl. She starts to talk about something that I'm not that interested in and inwardly I get a little irritated, knowing that my time with her is limited. I interject, trying to steer the conversation back towards my line of questioning. She takes the lead and the conversation starts to cover some really fertile ground. I'm too drawn in to take notes at this stage; this interview has started to become a conversation. I then glance down at the recorder – no red light. No red light! Oh crap – for how long?! I'm thrown. I vocalize my observations and apologize to the textile designer but ask her to keep talking. I get the damned thing going again and I frantically scrawl down all the fascinating aspects that I think I may have missed, while also trying to take in what she's now saying. She comes to the end of her reply and there is a short pause while I just catch up . . .

Done. Ok, what's my next question again, oh yes. We're back on track now but I am so annoyed. I can now not take my eyes off the recorder and have just noticed a 'low battery' warning. Oh that's just brilliant! I will it to keep going till the end. In my distraction, I initially miss that she has asked me a question. She notices and reforms the question. A question about my job. So I reply,

> I got a job as a lecturer, which I'm still doing, because I've always wanted to go into research. I was always more experimental, nothing I ever did was very commercial . . . . I was always into the processes so . . . I got obsessed with paper making, I got obsessed by . . . . I started off my PhD in flocking, I wanted to create some innovative surfaces, flocking with metals and you, know, sort of smart textiles. But along the path, my interest in the textile process, has sort of moved toward understanding the textile design process itself.

I suppose it's come round to this for me to understand myself, really, and my own place in the textiles industry. Why do I still call myself a textile designer when I don't sell anything? I don't even make anything anymore. I feel there is a way of thinking I know I share with people like you who do sell internationally, and designing for a commercial market, and that's what I'm trying to, sort of,

So, yeah. I was originally trained as a textiles designer but I'm not quite sure if . . .

Textile designer: You're not sure if you're still going down that road.

Or, kind of, which sort of position I'm in. Yeah, I just.

The battery dies. And I sense from her eyes that she feels that our conversation is coming to an end also. So I attempt some humour saying that even the recorder doesn't want to hear about me and she seems amused and a bit relieved that she's also no longer on the record. I ask her to complete the permission forms, as she does she says that she really hopes that I got what I needed. As most interviewees seem to do, she then starts to talk more candidly about her viewpoints, and again I try to make mental notes for the journey home.

She signs the forms and with an intake of breath, she looks at my rounded stomach and wishes me luck with the birth and the baby. I gather up my belongings, thank her for her time and the tea and we go back up the stairs and towards the front door, her husband comes into view from the kitchen and she quickly introduces me before he heads upstairs. As I say goodbye she tells me to pass on her best to our mutual contact and tells me to contact her again if I need to. She closes the door. I head back towards the station and feel totally incompetent of course – I'm such a rubbish researcher – I will always carry spare batteries from now on! On the other hand, however flawed the interview was, I feel that there were elements of what was said, by both of us, that offers both confirmation and further questions, and isn't that the point?

Almost two and a half years later, I reread the transcript (parts one and two!), dig out those scrappy notes I made at the back of my notebook, and remember. And I write . . .

Now seven years on again, this day is still so clear. Batteries – ha that dates it! Those questions at the end of the conversation now have an answer. Textile design research is what I am doing. I didn't know it then but those conversations are what unlocked that for me. Only through telling her story; my story; our stories, I was able to find this out. Yet, here I find myself on the frayed edges again. Not now wondering if I really am a textile designer but how I fit in as a design researcher. I am a feminist design researcher. Not making lived experience fit with the dominant ideas in all the books, but highlighting difference. I think they've used it in their own work. Such an affirmation. So now I find myself in a position which is more like a hinge, conjoining textile design with design research. I steal this metaphoric word 'hinge' from Adams, Ellis and Holman Jones (2008: 374). They describe autoethnography as a hinge – an instrument of transitivity. The point of flex and movement, the generative part, is the making of new design theory.

# 4

# Design, thinking and textile thinking

*[T]the absence of a significant interest from the chattier academic disciplines, the task of establishing such a discourse rests quite clearly with the textile community itself.*

(Gale and Kaur 2002)

Questions about the nature of design began to emerge in the late 1950s as a result of research into creativity, decision-making and management as well as advances in computer technology and artificial intelligence for problem-solving. The academic discipline of 'Design Research' developed as it became accepted that design involved a very specific and distinctive type of knowledge. Bruce Archer was a leading exponent of this view and was fundamental in the inception of the *Design Studies* journal and academic design research in general. In the debut issue of the journal, published in July 1979, Archer presented a paper entitled 'Design as Discipline' and put forward these questions:

> Can design be a discipline in its own right? If so, what are its distinguishing features? (What are the kinds of features that distinguish any discipline?) To what questions should the discipline address itself – in both research and teaching? What methodology does it use? What results – what applications – should it be trying to achieve? (Archer 1979: 17)

Archer's questions were devised to encourage a rationalization of the design process and focused on industrial design. On reading these questions, it occurred to me that if I were to add 'textiles' in front of the word design as used here I would find it very difficult to find answers to them in the existing literature

## Textile designing

*If textile design is to be studied in an attempt to understand its peculiarities,*
*then researchers should aim to systematically identify the nature of textile*
*design and the behaviour of textile designers.*

(Moxey 1999: 176)

Critical evaluations of the textile design process and the industry itself are few
and infrequently published. Colin Gale and Jasbir Kaur's 2002 publication *The*
*Textile Book* explored the range of personnel involved in textiles as designers,
craftspeople and designer makers, as well as outlining the industrial, historical
and global contexts for textiles, and they put forward an impassioned argument
in support of textiles and its associated industries as a worthy subject for research
and as a 'profession' cited at the beginning of this chapter. In their choice of
words they indicate particular characteristics, and therefore differences, between
design disciplines, and in doing so label textile design as quiet and unwitting
(Gale and Kaur 2002).

Rachel Studd's paper 'The Textile Design Process' (Studd 2002) sets out the
methods and activities textile designers carry out as they design. The paper
provided different accounts of the textile design process from the viewpoint
of a freelance textile designer to teams working within large corporations.
Her account and the various 'summary of design processes' she develops give
due regard to the variable factors that alter the experience for textile designers
within different industrial contexts. She also puts forward a basic flow diagram
of the structure of the textile industry and process which follows fibres, through
spinning into yarns, then dyeing; weaving, knitting or non-woven construction
methods; then printing and dyeing for a range of applications across apparel,
furnishings, technical and medical which are then developed into products for
retail or contract industries and ultimately in the hands of the consumer.

The essential structure of this diagram is simple and essentially correct, yet
several aspects of the activity of textile design have been omitted: in particular,
the significance of embroidery and other constructed textile and surface
embellishment techniques within textile design. Since the publication of Studd's
diagram in 2002, an even wider range of technical skills has become part of

three-dimensional textile surfaces. Military and automotive applications could be considered under Studd's label of 'technical' textiles; however, I feel they demand some consideration for their aesthetics as well their properties. Smart textiles have also been excluded. This field covers wearable, haptic and ambient technological textiles and contrasts with the technical textiles engineered by chemists, material scientists and industrial engineers.

Figure 1 is an adaptation of Studd's diagram. I have presented it in a non-prioritized list-based format, avoiding the 'flow diagram' style that Studd has used. This allows for the tracing of multiple paths through the textile design and making process. This table serves to illustrate the basic shape of textile design activity today.

While both Studd's (2002) and my own diagram illustrate the areas in which textile design activity is taking place across a range of industries, they do not represent what the design process entails for textile designers. For this discussion it is very important to remember the breadth of the textiles industry and how textile designers' fields of activity and therefore expertise have continued to grow.

The other significant detail from the table in Figure 1 is that textile designs, particularly commercial textile designs, undergo two levels of consumption. The first which takes places within the design industry itself and the second with the end user or consumer. This fact is key to developing conceptual understandings of textile design later in this book.

Previous studies of textile design process and cognition have mainly been pedagogical, involving students of textile design in higher education. Alison Shreeve opens up the conversation about knowledge in textiles in 'Material Girls: Tacit Knowledge in Textile Crafts' (Shreeve 1997) and in doing so emphasizes the need for more extended research in this area. Shreeve directly and consistently labels textiles as 'craft' rather than as a design discipline and closely aligns it to fashion. These labels and associations are clearly derived from the context of the research, based at the London College of Fashion and published by the Crafts Council. It may also be a legacy of the progression of the art-craft-design dialectic since 1997, when the paper was written. The aim of Shreeve's paper is to emphasize the pedagogical requirement to understand and value the visual, perceptual and tacit knowledge that is intrinsic in learning how to craft textiles.

In *The Representation of Concepts in Textile Design* (2000) James Moxey also

| | Fibres (Virgin or from Post consumer materials) Yarns Non-wovens | | | |
|---|---|---|---|---|
| | Natural / unprocessed Processed / dyed | | | |
| Textile design students Textile swatching studios Freelance textile designers In-house textile designers Designer-makers Craftspeople Own-label designers Hobbyists Research-led designers | Knitted Woven Non-woven Rapid-prototyping including 3D printing Engineered Bio engineered | | | |
| Material scientists Chemists Engineers | Fabrics Materials | | | |
| | Printed (digital & manual) Dyed Embroidery & embellishment Constructed & mixed media Laser-cut & etched Surface treatments (e.g. Washing, distressing) Smart technologies Surface pattern design Virtual technologies | Apparel Furnishing Architectural & Interior Automotive | Product for Retail<br><br>Product for Contract | Consumer |
| Issue based transdisciplinary research e.g. sustainability, ethics, social projects | | Technical & Industrial Medical & Biomedical Military Aerospace Digital technology | | User |
| | | First level<br><br>consumption | | Second level<br><br>consumption |

**Figure 1** Table of textile design activity (2020). Adapted from Igoe (2013).

to match the design process he has been observing with an established design process model. The outcome of this is unconvincing, as Moxey describes an iterative, free-form process where some students are encouraged to depart from the original design brief by developing their own briefs, but then proceeds in depicting a linear design process model.

Both Shreeve and Moxey seek to gain an understanding of textile knowledge and textile design by studying the actions and outcomes of students of textile design. This is clearly an important and valid aspect of the experience of being/ becoming a textile designer. However, it does highlight the requirement to extend the study of textile design to incorporate the variety of experiences and outcomes of professional textile designers at different stages in their careers. Dorst (2008) provides us with a seven-level model of expertise in the design profession. Within this model he specifies anomalies between approaches to design across the levels that help us to question the one-dimensional definition of the design process which has become so prevalent. Studd's work in 2002 gives some explanation of textile design in industrial contexts but does not deal with the cognitive aspects of textile design.

Shreeve's method is relational, adopting an ethnographic methodology, while Moxey adopts a scientific model, describing, analysing and classifying the tangible outcomes of the textile design process. Shreeve's study uses the (student) designer and their personal experience of the design process as the object of research while Moxey's study removes the designer from the research project, focusing solely on the outcome.

Pedagogical research has also been a key driver for research into textile design. In two studies exploring the relationship between textiles, engineering and technology (Kavanagh, Matthews and Tyrer 2008: 708; Kavanagh 2004: 3), the writers outline how education promotes three aspects of textile design: 'Discourse, Context and Process', simplified as 'What one wants to say, and to whom, and by what means'. They describe how education has become better at preparing students of textile design for working in textiles (the context) as a reaction to the criticism that discourse and process has long been emphasized. They go on to describe how, with greater contextual knowledge, their technical understanding of manufacturing processes has waned. In this example, 'discourse' can be read as the internal and external rhetoric as experienced by the (student) aims to engage with the entity of textile design in the context of design research theory.

The textile entity includes the textile designer and the discipline (Actor/s); the textile design object, the objective/design problem of textile design (Object); the manual and cognitive processes of textile design (Process); and the industrial, historical, political and cultural context of textile design (Context). These labels are an application of Kees Dorst's (2008: 5) argument that a focus on the process of design ignores the impact of the object, the actor and the context. I have added 'process' to this list to suggest that process is not the frame for these other aspects but rather is set in a complex relationship with them. This nexus describes the textile 'entity' I address in later chapters and correlates with an approach to the development of design thinking as 'sketched' out by Lucy Kimbell in her 2012 paper *Rethinking Design Thinking: Part II*. Kimbell facilitates a 'practice-centred' approach to design research. She suggests:

> Practice theories see the locus of the social not at the level of individuals and their minds, or in organizations and groups and their norms but as a nexus of minds, bodies, things, institutions, knowledge and processes, structure and agency. (Kimbell 2012)

And so, in asking the entity of textiles what it wants to say, to whom and by what means, the questions have a broader remit, requiring answers of a suitably epistemological slant. Studies by Rachel Studd and James Moxey (2000) both developed at UMIST, Manchester, UK, give a thorough description of the systematic design process for textiles, covering both students and professionals. However, systematic models of the design process have routinely been challenged by certain academics who emphasize the 'opportunistic' behaviour of designers in practice. Cross summarizes a range of studies that explore both systematic and opportunistic approaches to designing (Cross 2007: 109–12), highlighting the fact that the process of designing is difficult to define even though there are clear signifiers of the concept of a specific type of knowledge that design utilizes. He warns that 'the "cognitive cost" of apparently more principled, structured behaviour may actually be higher than can be reasonably sustained, or can be justified by the quality of the outcome' (Cross 2007: 116).

There are very few examples of research that have explored the phenomenon requires designers to 'import information into the problem space'. Moxey hints at how textile designers deal with ill-defined design problems when he describes concept generation for textiles as a combination of informed intuition, tacit knowledge and overt, market-rich data.

Studd (2002) provides an example of a design brief as used by a large UK-based textile company. It outlines the aims and objectives that the proposed collection must attain, including stipulations about the colours and fabrics to be utilized and the product dimensions to influence the repeat size, as well as the targeted consumer. Are these aspects merely technical and market requirements, rather than the articulation of an ill-defined design problem? Are they just setting the boundaries of the 'problem space'? Moxey and Studd focus on concept finding/generation and representation in response to a 'trigger' (Studd 2002: 43): can this trigger be seen as the design problem? Is it a more appropriate term than 'problem'? These studies do not yet fully interrogate the notion of the ill-defined design problem for textile design. They invite further investigation into the 'trigger' for textile design and initiate an articulation of the nature of the ill-defined problems textile designers deal with (see Chapter 13).

Ongoing academic discourse on the subject of textile design, thinking and practice has been evident in individual research projects of PhD students and academics. In 2010, researchers at Loughborough University founded the DUCK *Journal for Research in Textiles and Textile Design* in an attempt to publish online material of this nature. In 2013 it was relaunched as the *Journal of Textile Design Research and Practice*. In 2010 Bye outlined a 'new direction for clothing and textile design research' contextualizing the location of clothing and textile research in design research and as a site for scholarship and providing a historical account of the situation with particular reference to North American academia. In leading design journals such as *The Design Journal* and *Design Issues* and at international conferences we are seeing more contributions from textile practitioners and researchers. Textiles Intersections and D-TEX (*The International Textile Design Conference*) are developing as international forums for design research in the field of textiles as well as interdisciplinary special interest groups of larger colloquia such as the Experiential Knowledge Special Interest Group (EKSIG) of the Design Research Society, convened by textile design researcher Nithikul Nimkulrat. Research into innovative materials textile practice that could be applied in B2B contexts to support design-driven innovation for this specific market. Reflecting this premise back to textile design researchers, Earley, Vuletich, Hadridge and Andersen (2016) report on the role of textile design researchers in the development of sustainability solutions for a large fashion brand asking, 'What new skills and capabilities do textile designers need to inspire sustainable design innovation in large fashion corporations?'

This research, among others including my own (Igoe 2010, 2013), began to make textiles answerable to definitions of design as well as the issues design was causing and being confronted by. But in order to do this, what was required was some articulation or clarification as to what textile design is and does as a practice.

## Textile/design thinking

'Design thinking' is now a popularized and commercialized term but here should be simply understood as design cognition, the thinking associated with designing and a subject of study since the 1960s. There is, however, some agreement that the definition of 'design thinking' is now not clear and is not necessarily the most apt label for such a complex phenomenon. I refer here specifically to Peter Rowe's introduction of the term in his 1987 book *Design Thinking* in which he proposes that designers work on hunches and hypotheses and that the problem-solving action of the design process itself shapes the emergent solution (Kimbell 2011). I firmly make this distinction from 'design thinking' as a means of creative problem-solving heroicized by global innovation companies such as IDEO and which stands outside of this discussion of design theory. The co-option of the term 'design' in other spheres is problematic when not accompanied by rigorous critical interrogation potentially both on the outcomes of these processes and on the field of design itself but is beyond the scope of the publication. In this chapter, established concepts and theories of design are summarized and juxtaposed with the literature concerning 'textile thinking'. Here, I have selected to persist with the use of the term 'design thinking' to cover the embodied, cognitive activities of designers that are set in relation to their design process.

There are many good summaries of the development of design thinking as a of design research and 'thinking' in her book *Critical Fabulations* is essential reading for all design researchers. With gratitude to these authors, I can proceed here to locate and explain the development of 'textile thinking' in response to the phenomenal success of the notion of 'design thinking' beyond the world of design itself.

Textile design, in both educational and industrial contexts, is most predominantly focused on artefactual paradigms of design (Pastor and Van Patter 2011). There are clusters of research-led textile designers who are working in the field of service design and innovation – for example, Jenny Tillotson's work in 'scentsory' design. Fewer still working to bring about organizational and social transformation – Rebecca Earley and Kate Goldsworthy's work in sustainable design processes and business strategy (2017) or Anne Marr and Rebecca Hoyes practice research involving spaces, pattern and well-being (2016 and Sánchez-Aldana et al.) (2019) working with textile practice and memory. It is interesting to note that many examples of textile practice working towards social transformation or sociocultural impact are embedded within craft practice; contributing author Rose Sinclair's work (2015) on the Dorcas sewing clubs created by Caribbean women in the UK is a significant study of such impact. Textile design, in the way that design is more generally considered, is hard to place alongside positive social impact. Indeed, we are now recognizing the distinctly negative role textiles and cloth has on the environment and the people that make every aspect of them. An issue which now necessarily drives significant research in circular design methods and sustainable and responsible design, despite the industry being far slower to change.

The assertion that textile design is *design* is one of the foundational premises of this book. This may seem like stating the obvious but in the development of my doctoral thesis (Igoe 2013) I sought to find out why this notion was so difficult. In reviewing the established theories and concepts of design; the design process and cognition, what I uncovered was a theoretical canon heavily skewed by a blend of historically and socially gendered and biased factors compounded by disciplinary tenets. Scholars and theorists in and beyond design research such as Escobar (2018), Tonkinwise (2016), Kimbell (2011), Prado de O. Martens (2014) and Noel and Leitão (2018) have and are still voicing timely critique but their

Concurrently, in the UK, textile design scholars have been establishing a body of work to develop an understanding of thinking and making in a textiles context. Key texts from Anni Albers (1962) and Victoria Mitchell (1997) and later work by Sarat Maharaj (2000) as well as Janis Jefferies and Pennina Barnett in the development of the journal *Textile: Cloth and Culture* (2003–) helped to develop a forum for these academic concerns. In the mid-2010s Claire Pajaczowksa defined 'nine types of textile thinking' supported by notions of textility and characterized by the indivisible nature of thinking and making.

Design thinking and textile thinking – they sound so similar, don't they? But what lies between them are intrinsic epistemological differences set in place by historical ontologies of hierarchies of knowledge. The articulation of cognition as indivisible from the making has been the driver for the development of the term. As we know this knowledge-making is not something intrinsic only to textile practitioners (read Ingold on sawing wood), yet the way that textiles terms are so omnipresent in our lived worlds and languages; the notion is almost hiding in plain sight. The development of *textile thinking* or *textile design thinking* as a concept spans decades. Here I give a brief overview of this development principally in Europe and the UK.

In her 1962 book *On Designing* Anni Albers steers her discussion of making in general in and out of craft, design and art through her understanding of all these contexts and their relationship in the production of textiles. In doing so she establishes some of the defining traits of what has developed as textile thinking. Albers says,

'I believe that this direct work with a material, a work that in general no longer belongs to our way of doing things, is one way that might give us back a greater sense of balance, or perspective and proportion in regard to our perhaps too highly rated subjectiveness.'

She gives little credence to any distinction between crafted objects of art or mass-manufactured objects of design and offers a definition of the purpose of successful made objects as more for serving and less for expressing (Albers 1962: 64). She recognizes the collective input of makers-designers, artists, craftspeople as well as chemists and engineers in the development and production of objects but reiterates the need for all to be submissive to the materials to observe subservience in the process of producing objects. Albers metaphorizes the

She addresses modern forms of decoration with some apprehension, acknowledging that we sometimes seek the pleasing addition of *provocative beauty* beyond the restrained aesthetics of purpose through the application of colour and surface treatments. However, in imposing her own aesthetic, she also suggests that ornamentation and the strive for appending beauty to objects gives undue attention to the mediocre, hiding poor material choices, inciting a rivalry between objects.

In subsequent chapters, Albers outlines the significance of textile forms and their production in architecture, art and anthropology. Albers's collection of essays collated non-sequentially between 1937 and 1961 provides a foundation for my approach and the theories I propose in further chapters. Albers's contribution to writing on design as a textile maker is pioneering and erudite – diminishing notions of the heroic singular artist or designer in favour of the recognition of collaboration, commercial context and purpose. In the introduction to her later book *On Weaving* published in 1965 (Albers et al. 2017) she again sets out an invitation to others thinking and making through and with textiles and materials, saying,

'By taking up textile fundamentals and methods, I hoped to include in my audience not only weavers but also those whose work in other fields encompasses textile problems. This book, then, is an effort in that direction.'

Albers also focuses in on the goal of purpose and the conception of beauty in design and begins to question the role of the decorative alongside. The way she describes design realization as 'condensation' is poetic and relatable but certainly at odds with the concepts of the science of design that were being developed at a similar time. Without using the precise terms and learnt through her practice and own study, Albers describes hylomorphic approaches to making – the imposition of form to matter – and supports a return to privileging the connection between making, tools and materials, which has since been defined as *textility* chiefly by Victoria Mitchell and Tim Ingold.

Mitchell's essay from 1997 *Textiles, Text and Techne* proposes a textility of thought and matter represented through the etymological links of the three words that make up its title. She argues that, linguistically, we can understand the word 'textiles' not simply as an object but as a schema. And so, the construct of textiles is an approach to making knowledge manifested through the act of making itself.

disciplinary approach reminds us that making knowledge is world-making or more appropriately 'world-weaving'. He utilizes Deleuze and Guattari's theories of the relations between materials and forces noting that skilled makers intervene in the fields of forces and currents of material in the generation of objects. The indivisiblity of thinking, making, knowing with, in and of itself, bound up with the agency of materials themselves, becomes the premise of textile thinking. Mitchell and Ingold's development of textility permeates in the work of Dormor (2012) in her thesis concerned with art-making, philosophy and textile terms and practices. Kane and Philpott (2014) apply concepts of textile thinking to the development of sustainable materials within cross-disciplinary workshops, drawing on a range of textile processes for the purposes of fostering creative dialogue and innovation. To support this approach, they point out the application of 'textile modes of thinking' in the work of architects Frei Otto and Lars Spuybroek. Although they do not reference textility explicitly, what they discuss unearths epistemologies of textility in making and designing beyond the field of textiles.

My own doctoral thesis and an earlier article (Igoe 2010, 2013) sought to locate textile thinking in the field of design research theory. Theories of textility tended to enmesh a taciturnity with making and didn't sufficiently recognize the context of making as a practice of design in an industrial context. In one way, my work was a return to Albers's perspective but also differentially asserted the development of textiles as a design discipline with associated practices in relation to other design disciplines and not craft or art. This taciturnity was identified and explored as an obstacle to textile designers contributing to the development of the foundations of design research and theory and the zeitgeist of 'design thinking'. Through the work of Kane and Philpott, myself and Pajaczkowska (2016) who developed an understanding of textile thinking through nine examples of research praxis manifested through textile 'verbs' and drawing on etymological and linguistic links; a theoretical basis for textile design research was established and quickly became a shorthand for textile- and material-based research methods. Notable extensions of textile thinking can be found in Vuletich (2015) as she explores the role of the textile designer in industrial design contexts for sustainability goals; Marr and Hoyes (2016) who present textile thinking as an 'additional creative impulse for generic design thinking' that recognizes material agency of this as a conceptual framework. Lee, with particular interrogation to textiles in 'everyday contacts' and intimate social contexts, suggests that the essential relationality of textiles requires an ontological expansion of textile thinking into what she proposes as the *textile-sphere* – a 'mediatic environment' encompassing material and immaterial expressions of surface.

While 'textile thinking' has been a useful lever or metaphorical undercoat for emerging textile design research, through application without interrogation it often lost the etymological nuance of textility along the way. Textile thinking as a concept was established by the scholars mentioned earlier not as a justification for any lack of involvement with design academia and an invitation to carry on regardless but as a way of understanding a relational way of making knowledge through materials. Textile thinking with its roots in textility as the materialization of thought, language and expression and the agency and capacities of materials avoids addressing the context of designing. As if textiles are not objects of neoliberal commerce that exist and act in a complex socioeconomic structure. Design thinking, on the other hand, provides little recognition for designers who are material-led and for whom making is an effective way of thinking – where making is the key driver to their design process and where final outcomes and applications are routinely unknown. What was missing was a critical dialogue between these two types of thinking and in the meanwhile both terms, as is the way, have altered their meanings.

This book proposes and uses the term 'textilic practice' as an application of some of the premises of textile thinking in and beyond fabric-focused design outcomes. It is an effort to move textile thinking away from associations with design thinking and towards a more adisciplinary conception. Textilic practice in design uses a set of methodological processes or tools that focus on the materialization of creative expression through the agency and capacities of materials further explained in subsequent chapters. Materials can be understood as the 'stuff' of design – any kind of design. It is not giving form to matter but intervening between materials and 'forces'. In enforcing notions of textility rather than 'textilia', it attempts to secure an understanding of textilic practice that transcends disciplinary boundaries even manifesting in immaterial design outcomes.

Textilic design practice here is importantly contextualized epistemologically

# Mesh one

'Right – I want you to imagine it's the 1940s, it's a damp smoky dark railway station, this soldier's going off to war, the girl's standing on the platform with a bedraggled bunch of flowers, waving goodbye tearfully to her.'

She wanted those flowers, you see?

It was about responding to those sorts of poetic feelings, quite chaotically at the beginning. There must be a certain amount of interpretation on my part. I must understand and interpret that poetry and make it visible – realize it, in fabric; know which colours to pull out, how would they go; translate it into textiles; make it believable.

I accumulate information related to . . . whatever . . . and then there's the process of 'tidying up' and then responding to all that and very often all those three stages merge into one, so you're looking at things as well as organizing them at the same time as making something. 'In synthesis', that would be the best explanation. I tend to consume masses of information of all sorts and sources, mostly of visual but also text-based and initially it doesn't have any particular order. I might take inspiration for colour straight from photographs or an exhibition. So being inspired by a painting and seeing how that could be a design or being inspired by the new design by BMW and how that could affect the shape of a print or swimwear. I might then make patterns almost straight from visual research. Although what we're kind of taught is really to try not to just interpret your visual research, to try and actually do a stage further; that specific way of researching primary research, secondary research, then you pick out bits and put them together to create the design, although it's still quite organic. Somehow, I always talk about it as a process of osmosis. You've looked at something so long, or worked with it for so long, that suddenly it's coming out through your fingertips. I suppose I also think it's all about looking. Because I think that the biggest tool you've got in anything is your personal way of looking at something. Working in a design team, we'd kind of build up these little kinds of stories and themes and moods and ideas. Sometimes we didn't have very about whatever it might be. Then I just need to translate them into the computer as a design or colourway.

Alternatively, sometimes my process starts with a material; I take it apart, like a kid, and then find my own way of putting it back together again. I find it's a good way to get to know the material and understand what it wants to be. I like getting people to understand the technology that is available, and how it can be used. The materials research development company I once worked for needed somebody, really, who could transfer that kind of way of talking much more easily; I suppose it's that kind of link; being able to speak to certain people in a way that kind of enables them to gain enough information and to understand what it's all about but without kind of coming across in a too much of a technological way.

Now, working for a fashion brand, much of the time, the head designer brings in books or stuff that he thinks are interesting and he'll give it to me saying, 'Okay, this is the one I want to use for this season.' So I then come back here with their fabrics and colours and themes and play for a couple of days. I'm very much about feeding off another person's requirement and twisting it around in my head. Although it just can be a terrible, terrible experience because you don't know whether you're seeing things the same way or not. And sometimes you get clients that just even when you've done it to the colours that they've given you the swatches for, it doesn't look like the colour they want. It can be very, very difficult. Although I won't ever work with somebody who says, 'I want this here.'

An example of when it gets really interesting is when I was once working for two designers the same season, and they both gave me the same picture of a little boy with a tattoo on. And so I had to find two totally different collections from this one photograph, which was exciting. And also, if you are working for, say, seven different designers a season, then you've also got to have seven different styles. Different designers are known for their handwriting. So, I will often be asked to do things that are specific to my handwriting. You have to bend your taste to theirs without losing your integrity.

Often when the design is done, I realize it is really communicating visually what I wanted to say – although I didn't realize it would have looked that way. All of a sudden, all that research was pulled into one thing, even though I didn't consciously do it; that's when I realize it's good. I realize that I have created a feeling or a sense of it being romantic; or a feeling of being jazzy; or a feeling of taking you to the 1950s; or taking you to some place. I know people might not always get my work, but if they are attracted to it for some reason – they like the

# 5

# Translating and transforming

Victoria Mitchell states, 'Text and textile share common association through the Latin texere, to weave. These fragile references suggest for textiles a kind of speaking and for language a kind of making' (Mitchell 1997: 7). To 'speak' is 'to express one's thoughts by words' (Oxford English Dictionary). Textiles do not have words; they speak instead through a complex synergy of visual and haptic language, semantics (Andrew 2008). Nigel Cross (2007: 25) cites the work of Hillier and Leaman from 1976 in which they described designing as 'learning an artificial "language"; a kind of code which transforms "thoughts" into "words"', and state that 'They (designers) use "codes" that translate abstract requirements into concrete objects. They use these codes to both "read" and "write" in "object languages"' (Cross 2007: 29). Tacit knowledge is embodied in these languages or codes, the details of which vary across the design disciplines, feasibly offering researchers the possibilities of exploring non-verbal 'dialects' of design object language in the pursuit of the tacit knowledge of design.

I will not digress into the agency and nature of the textile object and its materiality at this stage. I wish to explore how the textile designer creates this communicative cloth – this semantic surface. Textile designers respond, translate, interpret and tidy images, words, stories, feelings, memories and objects in the development of their textile designs.

The qualification of a translator worth reading must be a mastery of the language he translates out of, and that he translates into; but if a deficiency be to be allowed in either, it is to be in the original, since if he be but master enough of the tongue of his author as to be master of his sense, it is possible for him to positing the textile designer as translator, I must consider what language they are translating 'out of' and 'into'? He encourages good translators to be a master of both. Textile designers respond to a varied range of visual, textual, auditory, sensory materials in their design process: a rich multimodal language. Taking Dryden's statement, the textile designer need not be a master of this multimodal language but must have a thorough command of the language of textiles in order to effectively convey what is being 'spoken of'.

Designers also describe how masses of information are collected, collated and 'consumed', some of it given to them by others and/or quickly 'vacuumed up' from visits to trade shows, exhibitions, online materials or gleaned otherwise from the visual environment. For the textile designer, the form of the original information has little significance; its inclusion is arbitrary. Direct and explicit communication is not the concern of textile design; it is precisely the expression of the 'sense', as Dryden puts it, within the language of textiles that is key.

The premise of emphasizing sensibility over content by no means belittles the textile designer as translator. The acts of vacuuming up, picking through and tidying which are part of the textile design process may not encourage deep and narrow expertise but rather a breadth of interconnected social knowledge.

Sherry Simon describes how translators must understand this connection between language and social realities. They must make decisions about cultural meaning in different languages and decide to what extent they inhibit the same significance. She adds that these decisions

> demand the exercise of a range of intelligences. In fact the process of meaning transfer has less to do with finding the cultural inscription of a term than in reconstructing its value. (Simon 1996: 138)

Hugo Friedrich's 1965 speech *On the Art of Translation* traces the history of this approach to translation to the ancient Rome of Quintilian and Pliny and describes its dominance during the European Renaissance. Friedrich also says:

> [T]he purpose of translation is to go beyond the appropriation of content to a releasing of those linguistic and aesthetic energies that heretofore had existed only as pure possibility in one's own language and had never been materialized before. . . . Its most striking hallmark is its effort to 'enrich'. (Friedrich 1965: 13)

Friedrich's speech is itself a translation by Rainer Schulte and John Biguenet, but used to describe the process of textile design. I enjoy the 'magical' qualities of this phrase, as if something ethereal has been given a form (through words or textile). What qualities does this attribute to the textile designer as translator? The textile designer doesn't just translate, she responds. The verb 'to respond' has a number of definitions and etymological historical origins (Oxford English Dictionary 2013), leading to nuanced understandings of the term. The most widely understood is 'to answer', but a more interesting one, and one which fits well with the idea of translating as 'enriching', is responding as 'to pledge back' (derived from the Latin *re-* 'back' and *spondere* 'to pledge'). If we consider that textile designers are pledging back to this multimodal language as they translate it and enrich it, a necessary level of trust is implicated.

Clive Dilnot, in his essay *The Gift*, recognizes this 'pledging back' in design as a form of gift-giving, but one outside of commerce, stating,

> [It] is the quantum of the designer's creative apperception of the conditions of human subjectivity, together with his or her ability to translate and embody this apperception into the form of the object and to offer it again to the potential user, that marks the designer/maker's 'gift' to the user. (Dilnot 1995: 154)

Dilnot skilfully triangulates the act of designing, with design as an agent of commodity and design as a subjective object. He highlights the relational properties of the act of designing as he uses the metaphor of giving gifts to explore the dynamics of design. He mentions the conative impulse designers feel – their implicit desire to make transformations in the world (transformations often driven by Western capitalist foundational structures) – and relates this to Adorno's description of gift-giving: 'Real giving had its joy in imagining the joy of the receiver. It means choosing, expending time, going out of one's way, thinking of the other as a subject: the opposite of distraction' (Adorno 1944: 42).

Dilnot is interested in how designed objects work between two people: the designer and the other. The designer takes the role of the gift-giver and the other (or consumer, first or second level – see Figure 1) is the recipient. He encourages us to momentarily rethink the connections that have been made between design and commodity. He reflects on the notion of the object as a commodity, where the gift-giver (designer) and recipient are disconnected through the capitalist structure. He argues that this scenario removes the sense of obligation from gift-giving and sets up an alternative notion of consumption definition of the pleasure-giving decorative arts and is a useful concept in distinguishing textile design from its close relatives in craft and applied arts, yet simultaneously maintains and recognizes the connection.

The notion of 'pledging back' that is developed through comparing design with translation is neatly captured in Dilnot's citation of Marx:

> I would know that I had created through my life expression immediately yours as well. Thus in my individual activity I would know my true essence, my human, common essence is contained and realised. Our production would be so many mirrors, in which our essence would be mutually illuminated. (Dilnot 1995)

This evocative passage offers a view into the pleasure, intellectual passion (Polanyi 1958) and relational mutuality involved in the design process: a process that deeply interconnects the designer with the object and user/consumer. It also allows a different reading of the innate impetus of designers – a passionate impulsion to communicate, translate and relate. 'The gift' poses an alternative definition of the character of design and the design process – one that involves the conative, cognitive and affective. In Dilnot's explanation, the gift is not the object itself but the latency of the object – a 'moment within' the object bestowed by the designer/maker. In support of this statement, he notes that most mundane objects contain this gift 'moment'. He adds that the moment is more perceptual that material. Textiles contribute to, and become embedded in, designed objects. In this scenario the gift-like moment of the textile is even more latent, as it does not constitute the gift-object in itself but contributes an essential element to it.

Dilnot (1995) differentiates between complex designed objects like computers and 'mundane' ones like 'clothes to keep us warm'. It can be understood that textiles would be categorized as 'mundane' in this context. While separating the two he also notes that mundane designed objects are no less significant than those he categorizes as complex. Interestingly, and in contrast, material culture scholar Judy Attfield (2000) called these mundane, everyday objects 'wild things'.

Dilnot affirms that the giver moves from a desire to give to an apprehension of the other's needs and desires.

> To put it in subject terms: as I anticipate the other's enjoyment and use of my object, and as I concretize those anticipated in an object that I choose/create, then I get the immediate pleasure and consciousness of having satisfied a real

designing ourselves'. He says that objects provide us 'artificially with what nature has neglected to bestow on us'. To work in this way, objects must be a convincing projection of our awareness of human existence, possibilities and limitations. Textiles, as designed objects, combining the tactile with the visual, can readily be understood as a projection of our base requirements of haptic, sensual, visual and perceptual stimulation. The designed object is a gift-like recognition of each other's base and complex needs and desires. The designer, or gift-giver, 'knows, and has understood, recognised, affirmed and sought to concretely meet our most intimate and human needs and desires' (Dilnot 1995: 155).

The notion of design as gift-giving described by Dilnot when set in context with neoliberal capitalism seems to be naive. Boehnert (2014) describes how the agency and perceptual abilities of designers towards addressing complex issues are denied by the capitalist design industry structured towards economic growth and the production of the new. White (2019) claims that the design industry in collaboration with large technology companies are creating and reordering social hierarchies.

In discussing textile design as gift-giving and as translation I focus on the cognitive acts associated with design. For textile design, due to its having first- and second-level consumers (Figure 1) within the design industry and the users themselves, this connection with social context has often been remote or lacking. However, by identifying this aspect through the development of making textile design theory we can connect design as gift-giving and translation through the notion of responding and pledging back. Both these scenarios illustrate a relational communicative act. The textile designer must, through their translation, pledge back to the original information an essence of its sense. They must also provide to the recipient a translation into cloth that meets their complex needs and desires. As discussed in reference to Dryden's comments on mastery of language, this again implies that textile designers need highly developed skills in expressing emotion and multimodal language.

To express emotion and sense requires trust. George Steiner described 'the hermeneutic motion' ('the act of elicitation and appropriative transfer of meaning') (Steiner 1975: 312) in four stages, beginning with trust. 'This confiding will, ordinarily, be instantaneous and unexamined, but it has a complex base. It

Claire Lerpiniere (2009) applied theories of hermeneutics to the 'inspiration' board, used widely by textile designers in the process of designing, describing how in practice these boards are used heuristically and have lacked academic and pedagogic investigation. The hermeneutic approach was applied to design by Donald Schön in 1983 when he framed it as a 'conversation with the situation' (Schön 1983: 79).

> There is initiative trust, an investment of belief, underwritten by previous experience but epistemologically exposed and psychologically hazardous, in the meaningfulness, in the 'seriousness' of the facing or, strictly speaking, adverse text. We venture a leap: we grant ab initio that there is 'something there' to be understood, that the transfer will not be void. (Steiner 1975: 312)

This initial stage relates to the notion of the 'creative' leap, the conative impulse towards making a change. Parallels between key theories of translation and established concepts of design have already been established, particularly in the research centre of Design Et Traduzione (DET) at Politecnico de Milano (Polimi), Italy. Baule and Caratti's edited volume (2017) provides a perspective on this notion from the disciplinary field of visual communication design. In this volume, Salvatore Zingale provides a detailed overview of models of translation (Baule and Caratti 2017: 71–93). He reminds us, 'The source text of design is usually an unstructured entity whose lines are blurred, open, exposed to uncertainty and incoherence, an entity striving to attain a finite structure precisely through design.'

In *Gender in Translation* (1996), Sherry Simon outlines a feminist discourse on the theory of translation. She highlights and recognizes the active agency of the translator and the participatory relationship between the translator, the text and the creation of meaning and considers Steiner's model, which, although beginning with trust, enacts itself through the perspective of masculine sexuality (Simon 1996: 29) (The other three stages of Steiner's hermeneutic model for translation are focused on aggression/penetration, incorporation/embodiment and reciprocity/restitution in the 'target' language.) Donald Schön's application of hermeneutics also utilizes interventionist metaphors, describing the designer's 'strategies' and his 'moves', likening designing to a game of chess (Schön 1983: 104). In contrast to Steiner's 'penetration' and 'entry' into the text, Gayatri Spivak describes an act of 'surrender' to the text. 'Hers is less a hermeneutical it with an understanding of tacit knowledge, using textile metaphors to help explain the scenario. She describes how, in translation, meaning 'hops into the spacy emptiness' between two languages and how the translator must attend to 'juggling the disruptive rhetoricity that breaks the surface [of the text] in not necessarily connected ways, we feel the selvedges of the language-textile give way, fray into frayages or facilitations' (Spivak 1993: 180).

> The task of the translator is to facilitate this love between the original and its shadow, a love that permits fraying, holds the agency of the translator and the demands of her imagined or actual audience at bay. (Spivak 1993: 181)

Spivak's feminist reading of the process of translation allows for an alternative subjective, relational understanding of design which contrasts with the notion of interventionist problem-solving. Spivak's mention of the love of the translator for the original text and its 'shadow' (the translation) acknowledges the subjectivity and the presence of the translator and connects with the notion of responding as pledging back (love, nurture, understanding). Spivak's use of 'frayage' or 'facilitation' invites an understanding of unravelling, disruption, entanglement as a positive and facilitative step in the creation of understanding or knowledge. Spivak's 'surrendering' is not to be misconstrued as a submission but rather as the necessity and willingness to be vulnerable to, and offer oneself up for, change and alteration in this co-emergent encounter. Michael Polanyi, in his writing on the creation of personal or tacit knowledge, captures the way in which Steiner's hermeneutics and Spivak's fraying and surrendering unite, in his concept of 'self-disposal':

> The satisfaction of gaining intellectual control over the external world is linked to a satisfaction of gaining control over ourselves. This urge towards this dual satisfaction is persistent; yet it operates by phases of self-destruction. This endeavour must occasionally operate by demolishing a hitherto accepted structure, or parts of it, in order to establish an even more rigorous and comprehensive one in its place. (Polanyi 1958: 196)

Aspects of Polanyi's theories on the tacit have been interpreted and popularized by Csíkszentmihályi as the notion of achieving 'flow' (1990). To gain control, you must lose control, so to speak. Returning to Spivak, it is a willingness to be located in the uncertain liminal spacy emptiness between.

the justification of freedom (over fidelity) in translation to 'unbind' meaning from language, speech and sense and to 'liberate' and 'recuperate' it (Benjamin 1923: 82).

# Transformation

Translations and translators have often been conceptualized as female and inferior in their relationship with the original text and author: the original is seen as generative, the translation as merely derivative (Simon 1996: 1). The expression 'les belles infidèles' has been used to describe translations as either faithful or beautiful, but not both (Chamberlain 1988: 455). Simon describes how feminist translation theory takes the traditionalist notion of fidelity or faithfulness to the text, author or reader in translation and redirects it to the process of writing itself. Applying questions of fidelity to an original in the process of translation towards the context of design relates to notions of unconscious and conscious variation. Philip Steadman (1979/2008) refers to Pitt-Rivers's 1884 experiments in successive copying as well as Henry Balfour's utilization of the activity as a research tool for *The Evolution of Decorative Arts* from 1893. He says,

> The origins or at least precursors of particular decorative forms were to be discovered by tracing them back through continuous series of always slightly differing copies. And as such chains of 'genetically' connected designs might begin and end with examples so widely different, that unless the intermediate links were known, it would not be imagined that they were in any way related. (Steadman 1979/2008: 99)

Following from said anthropological studies, it is widely understood that decoration has evolved through iterations of natural motifs and markings. Certain motifs have been successively copied and in doing so have changed form. Steadman sets up this copying as 'variation', which can be unconscious or conscious: either an attempt to reproduce the original as faithfully as possible or with some intent to alter or improve it. These concepts relate to approaches of translation; as such conscious variation corresponds to the feminist paradigm.

It contrasts newness with the comfort of familiarity – decoration as 'les belles infidèles'.

> In terms of pattern, individual motifs are totally transformed within the pattern as a whole, by the chance swaying of a dress or curtain. Pattern eludes, evades and troubles our gaze. (Graves 2002: 52)

A feminist reading of translation invites an exploration into the translator herself. Bogusia Temple describes how translators 'are often women paid for discrete pieces of work where they are not even acknowledged or named in the final written text (see also the invisibility of the translator by Venuti 1994). Their structural/social position informs their translation through the words that they choose to convey concepts but their influence on the text is marginalized and often ignored' (Temple 2005: 5.4). This situation is also synonymous with the role of the textile designer, often female, paid for the rights to one-off samples that go on to be incorporated into another design product, the input seldom credited and the impact often ignored. The correlation between the female translator and the female textile designer is significant in the development of a new understanding of textile design. The translator is further characterized by José Ortega y Gasset in his 1937 essay *The Misery and Splendour of Translation* (Ortega y Gasset 1937: 94), which views translation as a Utopian endeavour:

> To write well is to make continual excursions into grammar, into established usage, and into accepted linguistic norms. It is an act of permanent rebellion against the social environs, a subversion. To write well is to employ a certain radical courage. Fine, but the translator is usually a shy character. Because of his humility, he has chosen such an insignificant occupation. He finds himself facing an enormous controlling apparatus, composed of grammar and common usage. What will he do with the rebellious text? Isn't it too much to ask that he also be rebellious, particularly since the text is someone else's. He will be ruled by cowardice, so instead of resisting grammatical restraints he will do just the opposite: he will place the translated author in the prison of normal expression; that is, he will betray him. Traduttore, traditore.

Ortega y Gasset's depiction portrays a shy, humble person (as translator) full of courage, intention and aspiration yet 'marching toward failure' and betrayal (Ortega y Gasset 1937: 94). This characterization only holds true if fidelity examples of how translation has been used by female writers to find a voice, socially, politically and artistically. In regard to this, she describes translation as an 'intensely relational act, one which establishes connections between text and culture, between author and reader'.

In the integration of the metaphor of design as translation, notions of suspension and surrender to liminality in translation/design and the translator/ designer as rebellious bricoleur is the concept of a simultaneous movement towards and beckoning forth to the possibility of transformation. It requires the designer to imagine, embody and translate new possibilities, each of these activities involving the adoption of relational liminality: being between and at once in two situations.

In their contributing chapter, Elena Caratti and Daniela Calabi respond to and collaborate in the development of 'the translation paradigm for design culture'. Delving into their previous research developed from within the fields of visual communication design and architecture, Caratti and Calabi explore 'texture design' which they state clearly is texture including and beyond the textile. Texture design as a translatory mediator of place, territory, skill and cultural identity. For them, design (particularly involving textures) is a communicative act which makes memories accessible.

# 6

# The translation paradigm for design culture

Elena Caratti and Daniela Calabi

*Defined 'topologically', a culture is a sequence of translations and*
*transformations of constants ('translation' always tends to 'transformation').*

(George Steiner, 1975: 426)

Design and translation have a lot of affinities on multiple levels: not only for their conceptual foundations, values and principles but also and in particular in terms of processes of cultural transfer. The same evolution of the meanings associated to the word *translation* confirms the fact that this activity can be central in disciplines that go beyond the concept of translation in its literal sense (transposition of a text from a natural language to another).

We would like to assert here that translation is very close to the cultural, communicative, dialogic and creative dimension of the design discipline in all its declensions.

Indeed 'design is more than a socio-technical system. Design is a "cultural system" that, in producing and spreading innovation, . . . realizes a sort of *semiosfera*' (Penati 2013: 15); in other words, design produces multiple 'texts' (with an internal structure and a series of cultural external connections) that can be translated through different codes (visual, verbal, auditory, etc.). Design transfers ideas, cultures, philosophies, visions, experiences, images and imaginary of an epoch, of a context, producing, sharing and therefore 'translating' new meanings, new attitudes, new visions of the world.

To understand the concept of translation and its sense for design discipline, it is useful to take in consideration its meanings from the perspective of Translation Studies

In Latin we have further interpretations of the same term: the verbs *vorto* (to copy), *scribo* (to trace, to create, to compose) and *exprimo* (to model) are connected to a creative activity that promotes cultural and linguistic innovation. Instead, *converto, transverto* and *imitor* refer explicitly to the narrative translation that is finalized to the production of a readable text, without a faithful connection with the original one. In this case the problem of comprehension and content accessibility is central: a text (in all its forms) needs to be finalized to a specific receiving culture and entails a process of mediation between the cultures and sensibilities of the author and the receiver.

The use of the Latin verb *traducere* (and the substantives traductio, traductor) is relatively more recent (with Leonardo Bruni's work 'De Interpretazione recta', 1420) and includes three different categories of translation: the imitation or emulation (*metre en romanz, romançar, riducere*), the conversion or the explanation (*to turn, to deduce, to transmute*) and the re-expression or to render (*translater, transladar, transferir, to translate*). The same English word *translation* originates from the Latin *transfero, translatum*; basically it assumes a 'transit' between two levels of discourse, but over the time, the concept of translation has become more specific and it has assumed different and ramified meanings aimed at underlining its transformative, cultural, relational, cognitive, innovative potential.

The proximity between translation and design is particularly evident not only in communication design (Baule and Caratti 2017: 14) but also in other areas of design where immaterial and communicative qualities sustain and integrate with technological or functional properties translating social and cultural meanings. We can recognize in Translation Studies theories some principles and procedural criteria that can support design in its essence and cultural pluralism.

'Design is translation' starting from the *design process*: Torop's concept of 'total translation' (1995) is useful to find some analogies between the different stages of *translation process* with those of design process. The theorist, inspired from Jackobson's studies, defined the *translation process* in term of 'whatever transfer from a *prototext* (text of the sender's culture) to a *metatext* (text of the receiver's culture)' (Torop 1995). The steps, independently from the implied codes or transfer typologies, can be described as follows (see Osimo 2014, Kindle 65–8):

1. prototext analysis and elaboration of translation strategy;
2. content transposition;

This sophisticated model has many points in common with design process (Jones 1992: 61–73):

a. The first *analytical and divergent stage* of design process is finalized to de-structure the original brief (the prototext) to find not only criticalities but also design strategies and alternative ideas.

b. *Design transformation,* as Jones affirms (1992: 66), is finalized to impose a pattern that is precise enough to permit convergence to the single design. It is characterized by a series of transpositions that Torop describes in term of *interlinguistic, intersemiotic, intralinguistic translations* (according to Jackobson's definitions, 1959: 260–6) and moreover *metatextual, intertextual, intratextual translations.* In other words, as designers we realize a multiplicity of translational passages: from an idea to a concept, from function to forms, from contents to expression, from language to language, from techniques to techniques, from support to support (Baule and Caratti 2017: 269).

c. *Re-codification* process is a sort of a subcategory of design transformation and consists in the passage from a semiotic system to another (e.g. from verbal to visual).

d. *Design convergence* is the stage after the problem has been defined and the objectives have been agreed (Jones 1992: 68): the designer's aim is to reduce the secondary uncertainties (the semiotic noise or the residual) progressively until only one of many possible alternative designs is left as the final solution to be launched into the world.

e. *Design evaluation* (or translation critics) intervenes at the end of the design process; it contemplates the critic or the revision of the previous stages according to shared criteria.

The parallelism between translation process and design process allows us to outline some general principles that reinforce our assertions; design can be defined in terms of translation for different reasons:

– For the *attention to languages, their codes and translation models* (in all their declinations) that open unexpected possibilities of innovation and transformation. From this perspective new paths and new methods for design practice can emerge.

– Design, as the translation, is strictly connected to a process of *interpretation*

connected to the effort of the designer to find the best final solution through
a series of trials and attempts that can be only a compromise.

- Design very often proceeds, in parallel to translation, through the
categories of *imitation, selection, reduction* or *complementarity*, to express
the relationship between the *prototext* (text of the sender's culture) and the
*metatext* (the final output or text of the receiver's culture).

- In the same terms of translation, design projects need to have an *internal
coherence* and *cohesion* at syntactic, semantic and pragmatic level.

- Like translation, design is *target-oriented*: the cultural, geographical,
historical contest of the receiver is at the core of the project. The designer
and at the same time the translator put themselves in the position of the
final users to comprehend their norms, point of view and sensibilities. The
designer needs to predict a model of the possible final user who should be
able to interpret his choices.

- The principle of *translator invisibility* has, in some cases, a direct
counterpart in the *invisibility of the designer*, in his or her anonymity (Baule
and Caratti 2017: 19).

- Similarly to translated literature, design is a system that *plays intertextually*
with other systems and domains: from this perspective the project is
not an ended and closed product; it's a work in progress connected with
other projects, with other codes, with the society, the history not in a
deterministic way but citational (Barthes 1991: 181).

- In parallel to translation, design is developing its *metalanguage* as capability
to comprehend the meaning and the sense of its transfer practices. To face
various levels of complexity, designers must be equipped with theoretical
concepts that enable them to circulate productively. They also need a
methodology by which they can access meta-view points on various
perspectives including their own point (Morin 1977: 179).

- Through the translation paradigm design reinforces its *reflexive vocation*:
'every translation is an act of critical interpretation' (Neergard 2013: Kindle
439); at the same time, design through the translation paradigm can adopt
further analytical filters to reinforce its capability to critic culture, society,
the political system, against prejudices, conventions, stereotypes and
manipulations (Baule and Caratti 2017: 272).

in the common conscience as content looking for a form of expression: in this case, the designer invents and elaborates the proper form of expression that was lacking or inadequate before.

2. The translating activity in design presents itself as the ability to say clearly what was obscure and would have no other possibility of being comprehended. In this case, the designer is an interpreter of semiotically undefined contents and invents or elaborates a form of expression that makes those contents more accessible.

3. Design is an act of translation because it tries to say differently something already expressed, but that is semiotically weakened by the changing cultural contexts (or by historical, ethnical, geographical ones), but which could gain more strength if renewed and reformulated through techniques and instruments enhancing its expressive effectiveness.

This argumentation about the strict relationship between design and translation hasn't the presumption to be exhaustive; it's part of a wider and ongoing research that is finalized to the progressive construction of a gaze, of a design attitude able to conjugate linguistic and semiotic competences with the multiple complexities of design.

Texture design, too, is ascribable to a translation system where the combining principle implies the process of decodifying traces and the isolation of alphabet signs, the multiplication and succession of modularities within the principles of series and segmentation.

The meaning of the term 'texture' is related to the idea of a narrative plot which is *also* textile, but it's not the only acceptation. Every surface traced by signs, identifiable as a narrative of texture, gives back significant values, legible and interpretable as imprints on the skin of things.

In fact, it is possible to identify a closeness of meaning of the word 'text' (through which narration emerges) in the etymological and structural sense deriving from the Latin *tèxtus*, past participle of the verb *texere*, to the meaning of the word 'texture' and to the consequent concepts of 'narration' and 'communication', which are at the base of communication design.

Texture design manifests itself both as an ancient discipline and as a symbolic frame dense with traditions, as it belongs to vast historical and

However, through the recognition of writing and the richness of the meanings of the various textures, as well as through the observation of their diffusion and variety of design, it is possible to observe as follows. The intertwining of the signs on the surfaces (modular, chromatic and tactile) as well as the use of different materials and technologies affirm the evolution and transmission of the cultural identities of human civilization. Texture design is thus affirmed, from the earliest times, as an *instrument of communication of identities* (see Ciarrocchi and Calabi 2017: 23–32).

The use of textures is then transversal to the arts, and the study of texture itself has been approached from different points of view; today the contaminations between perception, design, historical, artistic and semiotic disciplines are evident. Thus, through texture, design reveals the interesting vocation to become an educational tool for creative disciplines.

The creative skills in the definition of the weaves and their variants build the semantic value of a texture: both when the textures are interpreted and reproduced through the most diverse printing technologies, with the use of analogue or digital languages, and when they decode meanings and symbolic perceptive characters. Once the domain of decorative art, texture has therefore played a unifying role in the visual arts.

Concerning the signs used in the fabrics, it can be noted that their combination is similar to the calligraphic compositions, both for the visual impact of the intertwining composition and for the symbolic force of the meanings. Consider, for example, the pages traced with the gothic typographic font 'textur', used in the printing of the J. Gutemberg '42 lines' Bible.

Textures, like calligraphy, are therefore material traces, which originate from sequences of gestures: from the hand that weaves the weft and the warp and the hand that generates writing. Roland Barthes (see Barthes [1994] 1999: 63) poetically reminds us how the hands, which in the prehistory of civilizations were mainly engaged in the locomotor function, were finally released from that task thanks to the evolutionary passage of the human being to the erect status, assuming then the fundamental commitment to *free words*. A liberation of the gesture, which however 'imprisons' the reader in the interweaving of the plot.

Barthes writes,

Epistemologically, the concept of intertext is what brings to the theory of the principal concepts, which are the articulations of the theory, all agree, in short, with the image suggested by the very etymology of the word 'text': it is a tissue; but whereas previously criticism (the only known form in France of a theory of literature) unanimously emphasized the finite 'fabric' (the text being a 'veil' behind which it was necessary to fetch the truth, the real message, meaning), the current theory of the text turns away from the text-veil and seeks to perceive the fabric in its texture, in the interweaving of the codes, the formulas, the signifiers, in which the subject is placed and defeated, like a spider that dissolves itself in its web. The neologism lover could therefore define the theory of the text as a 'hyphology' (hyphos is the fabric, the veil and the spider's web). (Barthes [1974] 1999: 6)

The textures therefore define a (meta) tactile/visual language that parallels the symbolic one traced by writing. The weft and warp design, which belongs to the material due to that transposition activity which is the *translation*, is 'texus': a narrative plot. This is because a translation from a tactile language to a visual language is possible, changing the support or the matter of the support, as it is possible to transfer the symbols from one composition to another, generating new meanings and involving the different forms of visual narration. Textures are therefore translations, with all the implications of meaning that this creative action entails.

The modular elements that make up a texture are mainly the result of combinatorial variations that create the appearance of the whole. The textures therefore make the *morphogenesis of the field* possible, a design of weaves that generates infinite variations of textures on the surfaces.

These weaves are made up of signs, calligraphies, colours, shapes and are essentially *micro-graphie* (Gaur 1997); they are figurative writings of a 'non-linguistic' semiotic space. A space where the carefully designed signs, then decomposed and recomposed, create interactions to form a 'text-image'.

In the design of surfaces, composition is therefore a special form of writing on the *skin* of things, where material values are added to the functional, meaning and perceptive aspects.

Texture design articulates two fundamental *perceptual forms of knowledge*: first, managing the interpretation of objects with the visual investigation of their surface, at a distance; second, returning an interpretation of the substance, of

In texture design, perceptive modalities interact and influence each other: 'synaesthesic perception is the rule' (Merleau Ponty 1945: 309 tr.it.). Therefore, it is possible to consider the *reader's* gaze as a sort of 'touch' at a distance. Because the layer of visible substance prepares for the haptic understanding of things. Because it carries out an action of mediation with those that can be defined as 'surface landscapes' (see Bruno 2014) able to offer perception the symbolic *translated* worlds composed of series of signs. Therefore, texture has a translative-*predictive* role as it anticipates and prepares to the understanding of meanings; it also has a role of *mediation*-translation, relating observer and object.

In textures, the possibility of experimentation in the field of visual cultures is constantly renewed. Therefore, from the point of view of studies on perception, texture design lends itself well to educational exercise; the study of the compositional process is particularly functional to basic design (see Calabi 2016).

The experiences of schools such as the Bauhaus, the School of Ulm and, in the United States, the experience with William Huff and his studies on tessellations in the plan (see Huff 1984: 36) reveal the fundamental importance of texture design for the development of *compositional skills*. Furthermore, the design of signs and the composition of the page combine well with the concept of *learning by doing*, typical of *basic design*, which is carried out with preparatory value within the principle of seriality (see Marcolli 1975: 98–107).

It is understood that the skills acquired through the study of textures are not only instrumental to technical exercise and visual grammar. The design practice aimed at composition (through the applied study of perceptive, formal and chromatic effects) activates, in the case of visual communication, the development of an appropriate *culture of the gaze*. It is no coincidence that the compositional choice of serial repetition is a widespread solution in graphics and, in general, in communication design. It's important to note, for example, how the profitable season of the 1960s brought out the linguistic abilities of the *form in succession*, with results of strong visual impact, catalysts of attention.

Among the great theorists and masters of basic design there is the Italian Attilio Marcolli who in his 'Field Theory' (see Marcolli 1971) highlights the value of segmentation of the field in the logic of seriality. In the signs arranged in a planar grid, the organization's methodological processes are recognized in reading hierarchies, consistent with the *Gestaltpsychologie*. Texture design, as design presents recursive syntax, due to its ability to generate infinite 'visual phrases' (see Chomsky [1966] 1978).

At the same time, it is rooted in studies on the organization of the perceptual field and the phenomenal units: seriality, modular composition, succession, perception, *deconstruction* (see Derrida [1967] 1998). Whenever a text is deconstructed, the structure of alternations and relationships generates new perceptual values, in order to adapt the result to the original expression. In other words, a *translation* of meanings takes place, the result of which is a 'metatext', a product that is semantically unchanged compared to the original text (see Popovič 1975) and therefore linked, from one or more pertinent levels, to the starting form.

The textures are *disassembly and reassembly*; they are born from a generative evolution of material form and meanings, which can take place by virtue of the translation principle and of that principle of segmentation of the field that allows reproducibility. The correspondence in meaning of alphabetic translations is shared by this form of visual writing. Textures are therefore abstract configurations of a narrative told through images (Veca 2007: 191), in which a 'morphogenetic' type of writing, whose form is in potential transformation arising from the relationships between the plots, dominates. Texture design invites the creation of a text-writing whose body is made of graphic (type) modules; it produces narrative and graphic text; it connects texts and hypertexts; in the page, it relates semantic writing and image. The textures are poietic design (from the Greek *poiein* which means *to do*) and estesìa (sensitivity, perception).

Texture is therefore a means, an interface, a medium whose value is often rooted in the cultures and territory of origin. The recurrent motifs, the shapes and the colours make it possible to identify the traditional, geographical and cultural origins expressed in the symbols. They charge the modularity of *sinsemantic meanings* that can be interpreted completely within the value of the whole. When the form of writing enters the memory it is translated into identity and sense of belonging. In this case, the design of surfaces makes immaterial traditions accessible. Through colours and signs, the textures reveal the artistic influences, the history and the origins to the expert. Like a story, texture is open to the interpretation of those who know the symbolic language. Signs that translate signs, therefore, in accordance with the concept of 'unlimited semiosis' by Charles S. Peirce (Peirce [1931–58] 1989), reconfirming the analogy between transposition and identifying translatability. Many forms of craftsmanship knowledge of the Mediterranean Basin express this design sensitivity through texture design, a translative point of view of tradition and culture. Therefore, through the study of constants and differences between signs, it is possible to interpret the intrinsic identity inherent in surfaces. With the assumption that every translation derives from a 'prototext', meaning from an initial text, the original reference here are the artistic cultures of the places where they are rooted.

While the material and workmanship return a global identity also linked to the common historical, morphological, geographical and geological features of the Mediterranean countries, the 'aesthetic' – and therefore perceptive – elements of the surfaces define those 'immediate identities' typical of local cultures. The whole set of signs that characterizes surfaces often translates local aesthetic characters; it explicits the belonging to a specific place thanks to these immediately perceptible aspects that offer codes for decoding. Texture design lends itself to these intersemiotic passages, without losing the semantic connotations of the context and the environment that generated them. Texture design, therefore, intended as the *design of cultural translations.*

As in the translation process, design also identifies a practice in the transition from one language to another, from one morphology to another, from one world of meaning to another. By translational analogy, it is the intersemiotic and, in general, perceptive passage to a visual language – found, for example, in the narratives that migrate between cultures and media, which tell of techniques and technologies, pigments, styles and historical roots.

It can be said that the design of surfaces of artisanal artefacts translates into visual forms from the anthropological space. The surfaces become the space of communication and exchange between worlds that express cultural characters with different signs. Texture, therefore, is intended as a decisive passage that spreads the character of identity and belonging, expliciting it in the process and sometimes hybridizing and stratifying signs of different origins.

In this case the textures are intended as 'cultural fabrics', as forms of writing born of design and historical crafts that respond to the traditions of the places where they are rooted, which make the memories accessible. Therefore, texture design represents a means of mediation between languages that express

These reflections lead texture design to translation design (see Torop [1995] 2009) – a translation that, from an interdisciplinary point of view, identifies a nucleus of theoretical principles and consolidates itself as a *communicative act*, as a linguistic transposition with translation rules and norms.

## Notes

The concept of semiosphere was introduced by the Russian semiologist Jurij Lotman in 1984. As Osimo asserts, referring to Lotman, semiosphere can be conceived in terms of a universe of signification in which the various spheres (from the individual to the continent) communicate with each other through membranes embodying the culture of boundaries or cultural differences (Osimo 2015: 11).

Jackobson (1959: 260–6) extended the concept of translation beyond the common sense of *interlinguistic transfer* between two natural language systems. He expressed two additional categories: *intralinguistic translation* or reformulation: interpretation of verbal signs through other sign of the same language (and same code); *intersemiotic translation* or transmutation: interpretation of verbal signs through non-verbal signs (the two systems differ in term of code).

# Mesh two

People respond to textiles quite badly, I think. Even at college it seemed to be quite a 'low down' course. I say to people I do textiles – oh what do you sew, do you make clothes, and it's like, no . . . I actually explain to people textiles is really broad and quite sculptural and it's quite three dimensional and you can use, you know . . . doesn't have to be fabric, it can be metal, plastic and what have you. People just don't get it. I remember a few of the experiences where you're presenting work to an audience that the majority of them are engineers, textile engineers and it goes completely over their heads, they're looking at you like you only do pretty things. They see us as people who make things look pretty. It seems like a fluffy subject. Once you say 'textiles' people get all these different stereotypical images in their mind and it's hard to get them to understand what you're about. 'Yeah, you've got big jewellery on, you must be a textile designer.' But you can't really define a textile designer.

Textiles is moving to technology to try and rid that idea, which I applaud. It makes an awful lot of sense, obviously. But the whole making of beautiful fabrics isn't a fluffy thing. It's really not. And it's that that we've got to sell/explain.

It's the whole male/female thing, it's like textiles is predominantly female and then, generally, like product design is mostly male and they'll design something like a textile, big panels that kind of fit together, and they're like look, they're textiles and I looked at it and think, god, it's a bit crap, and we could have done it millions of years ago, kind of thing, and yet it's awarded 'best use of textiles' and it's just . . . shocking. It really drives me up the wall. People don't seem to, kind of, seek out textiles. If it's done by some male industrial designer who's, you know, great or whatever then it's fantastic. Textiles is not thought of that highly. Textiles isn't obviously completely forgotten but I do think it is up to us, the textile people, to really push forward our ideas and our techniques and really kind of get ourselves out there, I think. We all know what textiles is, whereas most of the other disciplines, it seems to me, are constantly evolving, whereas textiles seem to be, kind of, stuck. It's like, we're textiles . . . shitty textiles . . .

think I could ever get to the point where I could ask somebody else to take on what I'm doing. I like the process. I think I like the structure of weaving because it takes some of the variables away. Like painting is pretty scary on a blank canvas. I like to push that structure, work within a structure like that. I don't think I'm an artist. I'm a designer and I'm a designer craftsman and designer maker. I don't know exactly which. It changes. I just love fabric and materials.

And when you've been working with something for so long it becomes less deliberate and somehow the work for me takes on more of a life and I know when to stop something too, because I know then it's just becoming . . . . I can't sort of describe the process but I seem to be thinking something in my head but what I'm doing I kind of later realize that, oh, it's kind of linked but it's not on purpose.

I didn't really appreciate, maybe . . . didn't appreciate my creativity until you come into the environment of a different discipline like this. I realized that the way that I think is completely different to how they think. Actually my input is very important in terms of that.

Dealing with people who probably know little about textile designing – they're mainly fashion designers so they don't know what's feasible to print, particularly – they'll buy something that fits in with their look, their style, their direction. There's an appreciation of the beauty of it but no understanding of the work involved. Textile design in the textile studios, in the way it's working now, is the most daft situation – you do the stuff in the way that a fine artist does stuff, and then you go out and you say: 'What do you think – do you want to buy it? Is it right for you or is it not?' So it's a very bizarre situation . . .

I don't particularly like going to trade fairs. I hate it, it's reactive. I like to ring someone up and make an appointment and go and see them. It's a private thing. As a studio we generally just don't do particularly well in the trade fairs but you have to go because you have to show your face and get new customers. I'm not a hard-sell salesperson. I'm not a salesperson at all, you know. I'll try and persuade people that they want things but basically if it's right, it's right and if it isn't, it isn't – they'll come and buy it. I hadn't realized how good you had to be at selling as a designer in that scenario, that was a new one on me. Maybe that's related again to the idea that we're behind everything and that we need to sell ourselves to these other fields of design in order for our work to go anywhere. Textile designers are shy people, they don't like to be on stage, they prefer to stay behind the scenes. But you have to be utterly convinced that what you're doing is

You're always working on two seasons because somebody is always looking for something different . . . and you're trying to show them new designs all the time or a new enough look that convinces them. it's good to put your work in different contexts. It's just like working for a client really, I suppose.

Really early on, I worked with a fashion designer, creating key embroideries for his collection. And yet I haven't even got a seat, I'm standing at the back. And on the piece of paper on the chair it often says, 'Thanks to so and so and so and so for the hair. Thanks to so and so for the tie.' And at the bottom it says, if I'm lucky, 'Thanks to me for the embroidery or textile.' But never my full name. 'Cause they don't want somebody else to come along and use you.

I did challenge it with the company. They said, 'They want to buy this label, I'd be a fool to diffuse it with your name and you'd be a fool to diffuse your name with my name, because they would buy less, because they want me, you know?' So yeah, fine. Let's carry on, because you can't buck it, you can't fight it. Because that was it. But I would really love textile designers to have people backing them to say, 'No, your name must be on it.'

And I think that when you get textile designers who've actually done well, whose names are really well known, they are people with either fantastic business backing or have that character of showmanship. I often think that textile designers work like this, and fashion designers work like that. We all get off on that little mark, and we're really happy if we've done that nice mark, we'll go to bed really happy. Still, there are some people that say, 'Oh, don't you think it's a shame that you're not the name?' Sometimes yes of course I feel like that, but often I'd hate to be that name and I'm happy with what I do and where I am.

I think us textile designers tend to be, I don't know whether it's we're the type of people or whether it's the kind of, the history of it, but we tend not to be nearly as confident about what we do as other design disciplines. There's that whole kind of side of fashion which is about showing off and about being, you know, a bit more theatrical or a bit more, you know, kind of, look at me, I suppose. I feel that we're quieter people, it's not all about me, me, me, working with fashion people, they are a bit pushy, more pushy. Textile's kind of quietly working away, kind of, coming up with these things. There's a very different . . . it's a different characteristic, it's a different kind of person that wants to do that. It's a different kind of person that wants to, you know. . . . My students describe how when collaborating with individuals from other design fields they kind of feel that they're producing cloth for them and that it's an unequal partnership, if you like, and that . . . they seemed to be kind of resigned the every-day that we're kind of so used to it and it almost, you know, stems back to lots of domestic practice and people hand-knitting and those sorts of things. And because it is, in a sense, a supplier to other industries. It is, you know, the stuff they use, so because it's not the ultimate end result, you know, there isn't the same starriness or star designer sort of thing associated with the textile designer because it always then gets developed or moved on into the product or into another kind of area. I think it is seen by others as a service industry, especially the fashion industry – shouldn't say that at all. With my career this is one of the real bugbears. It shouldn't really be like that but it is, because fashion's demands are so much different to ours and the hierarchy and the politics behind it are so complicated, you know. It's incredible. We're a service provider for all of those different design disciplines, and so it, you know, it affects how all of those different areas work. You do end up being the slightly lower down one. You have to just be prepared for that.

For me, here, it's all about . . .it's not about trying to surprise so much, it's about trying to fit in with what someone else's idea is. It's trying to give her what she feels. You must recognize what's needed for who you're working for. I'm closely informed about what they need in the collection and what's going on in the collection so I can fit with their themes. I don't as such have my own range. I work across all teams. It's quite unique but it also means I don't actually get involved in kind of the selection process. That's what the garment designer does. So at the end of the day they are kind of more accountable for the range as such. I'm just kind of a tool for them really to put it together, I'm like a resource.

# 7

# A story of hard and soft

## Modernism and textiles as design

Pennina Barnett provides an alternative understanding of the phenomenon of metramorphosis as developed by Ettinger. She describes 'soft logics' in reference to Michel Serres's concept of 'sack thinking' (Barnett 1999: 183). For Barnett, this paradigm sits beside the binary ideology (Serres's hard, box thinking) of 'either/or' and invites multiple possibilities, encouraging 'and/and', permitting 'the opportunity to be oneself in a new way'. Serres (1985) talks about the liminal threshold between hardness and softness, how one gives way to another. Soft logics and their significance to an understanding of textile design thinking require considered analysis, which I will certainly address in Chapter 13, *Making, problems and pleasures*, but for now I wish to use Serres's concept of a relationality between hard and soft to explore a narrative providing a metaphor for the socio-historical context of these ideas.

I am going to take Paul Scheerbart's 1914 novel *The Gray Cloth* (Scheerbart 1914) as a reflection of the contradiction between textiles design as the ideal medium/tool for the modernist message and how its associated thinking was marginalized within the universalism of the movement. This is inextricably paralleled with the prevailing position of the feminine and feminism in modernist thought (Sparke 1995).

I first came across Scheerbart's name in Richard Weston's introduction to the fourth edition of Niklaus Pevsner's *Pioneers of Modern Design* (Pevsner 2005: 9). Weston critiques Pevsner's original text, commenting that no account of early modernist architecture would now ignore the expressionist circle of Bruno by its narrative of the relationship between coloured glass and grey fabric, architecture and clothing, male and female, hard and soft.

Conceived and written as an expressionist novel, at the dawn of theoretical modernism, the novel is set forty years later, at the watershed of what would become popular modernism. It begins by introducing the hero-architect and coloured glass enthusiast, Edgar Krug, seemingly loosely based on Scheerbart's friend and collaborator, Bruno Taut. We meet Edgar, and his impulsive and immovable opinions, at a showcase of silver sculpture, in an exhibition hall of coloured glass and iron near Chicago which he had designed. The characterization of Edgar is accompanied by the sound of the organ, expertly and passionately played by his future wife, Clara Weber. Edgar is annoyed by the fashions of the women attending the event, feeling that their clothing choices showed a lack of respect for his coloured glass walls. When he eventually meets Clara, the talented musician who had created the phonic atmosphere that had amplified the effect of his architecture, Edgar notices that she is wearing an outfit of grey fabric (with 10 per cent white), which he feels is the most complementary clothing to be worn within his colourful glass buildings. Almost immediately he proposes marriage, with a clause that Clara should only ever wear this combination of grey and white. She instantly accepts, and they are married that night. The novel then travels with Edgar and Clara on their glass airship as they visit his various architectural projects around the globe. Throughout the novel, Clara is encouraged by other women to break the marriage terms or at the very least subvert them in some way. While the novel focuses on Clara's clothing, it is not her clothing style that Edgar is concerned with but the cloth from which it is made – its colouration, patterning and textures. Edgar Krug not only stipulates that Clara must wear grey cloth with 10 per cent white but that her clothing should not be made from velvet or silk (Scheerbart 1914: 10).

The *Gray Cloth* was the first of Scheerbart's novels to be translated into English, in 2001. Reiterating Weston's comment (Pevsner 2005: 9), John Stuart (Stuart 1999: 61) describes how architectural historian and theoretician Reyner Banham lamented Scheerbart's exclusion from the canon of literature on modernist architecture, despite being a key influence in the avant-garde art and architectural correspondence circle The Crystal Chain, active in 1920, which included Walter Gropius and Taut (Stuart 1999). Walter Benjamin expressed his esteem for Scheerbart's writing, and Scheerbart's 1913 novel *Lesabéndio* directly

Written within the German expressionist oeuvre, Scheerbart's fantastical, science-fiction-based story about modern architecture was characteristic of the utopian thinking associated with the movement and typified in the glass architecture of Bruno Taut. The onset of the First World War and its economic and psychological impact on the German people, and also the wider global population, provided the backdrop of disillusionment that saw the utopian emphasis on self within expressionism evolve into the concept of universal truth of modernism.

The novel's influence on architectural theory is certain, although arguably understated; however, its treatment of clothing, fabric and colour has certainly been ignored. Reading this story as a textile designer, it elicited frustration in me. The textiles were being denied their decorative, pleasure-giving role by virtue of the dominating concepts of architecture. At play is Scheerbart's humorous and ironic tone, often rejected or overlooked by many (including Benjamin) (Stuart 1999). As John Stuart states, in his introduction to his translation of *The Gray Cloth*, Scheerbart courts the discussion about the relationship between architecture and textiles initiated by Gottfried Semper some sixty years earlier.

> He was, moreover, able to relish the rich irony of these antagonistic positions by proposing in *The Gray Cloth* that contemporary women's outfits be fixed and unchanging – and thereby modern – while architecture was colourful, vibrant, and expressive – and thereby fashionable. (Scheerbart 1914: xxxvi)

Interestingly, in his paper *Unweaving Narrative Fabric: Bruno Taut, Walter Benjamin, and Paul Scheerbart's The Gray Cloth*, Stuart uses textile metaphors to describe his own analysis of the novel and likens Scheerbart, as storyteller and thinker, to a weaver:

> Rather, I would argue, Scheerbart wove a narrative fabric . . . . Moreover, in the process of unweaving this fabric, we gain knowledge not only of the culture that produced it, but through its interpretation of the architecture culture of which we are a part today. (Stuart 1999: 69)

He also notes Scheerbart's interest, at the time of writing *The Gray Cloth*, in 'interactions and negotiations between fantasy and reality'. Statements such as these invite comparisons between the means of conception and creation of *The Gray Cloth* ... ... (specifically as narrative) and that of cloth itself narrative as a mediator between utopian ideals and the constructed realities of gender, fashion, materials, human interaction, and architectural experience at the basis of twentieth-century modernity' (Stuart 1999: 69).

And so as I explore the literal story, considering how soft materials (textiles) are suppressed in favour of the hard (glass architecture) in this imagined version of the modernist world, I also apply it as a metaphor. This allows me to explore the interrelationship of Clara and Edgar; Clara as a representative for textiles as feminine/matrixial and for feminism in the modernist context and Edgar represents the domination of the modernist notion of universalism and the metaphorical patriarchal guardian of the hierarchy of the arts.

The *Gray Cloth* illustrates perfectly how the aesthetics and design of textiles and female clothing were subjugated to architecture within the modernist movement. Stuart states that by the time the novel was written, several leading Germanic architects (Van de Velde, Hoffmann and Behrens) were designing women's garments as part of a complete design environment (Scheerbart 1914: xxxv), or 'Gesamtkunstwerk'. Gesamtkunstwerk can be understood as meaning 'the total work of art': it is a term that was used prominently by composer Richard Wagner and applied to modernist architectural theory in the teachings of the Bauhaus. Textile design was considered to be an ideal medium for developing the concept, due to its ability to be mechanized and its versatility as a creative medium.

> Modernist textiles – because they functioned on so many levels . . . were inherently engaged in modern life, they occupied actual space in the gallery, home and showroom, they transformed the human body, and they changed the face of industry. As such they constituted a vital element in developing conceptions of the total work of art. (Gardner Troy 2006: 16)

Gardner Troy (2006: 13) describes how the concept of Gesamtkunstwerk permeated all aspects of textiles – its design, theory, production, marketing and consumption – which situated textiles at the heart of the modernist movement, allowing artists, designers and theoreticians to explore gender roles, primitivism, abstraction, constructivism, new technologies and materials and consumerism. Some might say that the very permeation of the ideology of Gesamtkunstwerk into textile design both highlighted and subjugated some of the defining characteristics of the discipline. Its functional characteristics – adaptability, transferability and versatility – were exploited, while the typical majority of women students were directed into weaving workshop, so much so that they became known as the 'women's workshop' (*Anni Albers: A Life in Thread* 2019). Gardner Troy (2006: 15) describes textiles as an 'object of neglect' within modernist theory and attributes this to two main reasons. The long association of textiles with the work of women in the domestic sphere, societal gender roles and a lack of access to education for women has seriously impacted on the inclusion of textiles in historical and theoretical inquiries. Gardner Troy also explains how the ambiguity of the textile medium itself has been detrimental to the development of an understanding of its significance in the history of art, design and craft. Textile design employs so many varied techniques and skills and is so commonly is given an auxiliary role, surreptitiously used to form other designed objects, that it is difficult to categorize and easy to overlook. In *The Gray Cloth*, the highly talented Clara subjectively experiences or exhibits these phenomena, and as such I attribute to her the entity of textiles at the time of modernism.

> I came to the Bauhaus at its 'period of saints'. Many around me, a lost and bewildered newcomer, were oddly enough, in white – not a professional white or the white of summer – here it was the vestal white. But far from being awesome, the baggy white dresses and saggy white suits had a rather familiar homemade touch. Clearly this was a place of groping and fumbling, of experimenting and taking chances. (Anni Albers in 1947; Albers 1962: 36)

Albers's description of the chaste 'uniform' of the Bauhaus relates well to Clara's grey garb. Both examples implicate that too much colour, pattern and texture in clothing is sullying and immodest, an obstacle for the eye and mind in its search for the modernist 'truth'. Albers remarks that she found this scene initially odd but accepted it. Clara, through her modest clothing, serves as a vehicle for her husband's version of Gesamtkunstwerk. Rather ironically, it is the lack of colour in her dress, its rejection of 'fashion', that encourages her husband's clients to accept more colours in their building. Edgar is adamant that his architectural concepts should not be overshadowed by the immediacy and sensuality of the textiles of fashionable clothing.

> The clothing must step aside for the architecture. Under no condition is it to compete with the architecture. Only gray fabric is allowed. (Scheerbart 1914: 9)

Stuart states, 'The dichotomy between fashion and architecture in *The Gray Cloth* may be seen, though, as opposed to the ideology of the Gesamtkunstwerk' (Scheerbart 1914: xxxvi).

Clara's acceptance of Edgar's marriage terms can be read as a metaphor for the acceptance by the textiles discipline of the hierarchical nature of the modernist movement, favouring architecture over textiles, with architecture governing the design and application of textiles in clothing and interiors. Ironically, Edgar's beloved glass is in fact strengthened by a textile structure: a strong mesh reinforces some of his buildings:

> Between the two sheets of glass lies a thick wire mesh and the whole thing is melted together. (Scheerbart 1914: 24)

An expression of Semper's theory of the textile origins of building in Scheerbart's notably ironic style, perhaps? Rebecca Houze (2006) argues that it is precisely Gottfried Semper's theory of cloth as a symbolic building material, and principally his concept of 'Bekelidungsprinzip' – the notion that a building's significance depends on its 'dressing' – which influenced this move to consider cloth and clothing as essential to a complete and modern architectural space, or Gesamtkunstwerk. Mallgrave (Semper 1851: 1) suggests that Semper's vision of Gesamtkunstwerk was one where 'architectural masses became enlivened and shaped, as it were, by ornament, colour, and a host of painted and plastic forms'. Houze (2006) identifies the architectural designer and cultural commentator Adolf Loos as another follower of Semper's theories. His critiques of 'ladies' fashion' and ornament can be read as an expression of his personal interpretation of 'Bekelidungsprinzip'.

In her essay *The Textile as a Structural Framework* Houze takes Semper's concept of textiles as architecturally structurally 'significatory' (Houze 2006: 298) and uses textiles as a conceptual structural framework to develop an understanding of the cultural life of Vienna in 1900. Here, I am examining *The Gray Cloth* by considering textiles as primarily significant to both the architectural narrative of the story as well as its conceptual framework in the expressionist roots of modernism.

It is revealed later that Edgar's own workrooms at his home at Isola Grande were not walled by glass, but by reinforced concrete, lit from above and applied with all manner of textiles, decoration and natural materials. Clara's friend Käte silk on the walls. Fur I like less on the walls. The colourful hummingbird feathers are also interesting on the solid wall. (Scheerbart 1914: 107)

This information aligns Edgar Krug with that of modernist architect Adolf Loos. Loos's ascetic exteriors belied the interior spaces, which were 'dressed' with various textile and material surfaces (Houze 2006).

It is better to have a colourful house than colourful clothing. The former makes all of life colourful, while the latter only serves vanity and makes away with money that should be for building houses. Edgar was right about The Gray Cloth. (Clara Krug, in The Gray Cloth. Scheerbart 1914: 86)

This excerpt emphasizes the notion of textiles and clothing as commercial, trivial items, while architecture aspires to higher objectives. Andreas Huyssen (1986) states that modernity classified high culture as masculine and popular or mass culture as feminine. Clara's acceptance can be seen as metaphorical of both the submission of textiles to the modernist tenet and, more broadly, of textiles as feminine, submitting to the patriarchal structure of the design world. It appears that it was the very practitioners of textile design, being predominantly female, who prevented textiles from being the ideal, modernist design practice.

If we consider the female characters in the book, we can see that Scheerbart generally develops them as talented and artistic. One of the focuses of Scheerbart's novel is on Clara's communicative skills, both discursive and musical. A large proportion of the text is given over to Clara's telegrams to and from her friends. Her organ playing 'roars with stormy rhythm' (Scheerbart 1914: 4) and she is able to subtly influence Edgar's clients' design choices. She is venerated wherever she goes and makes friends easily, eventually becoming famous in her own right. The points at which Clara subverts the marriage contract correspond with her playing music and her meetings with groups of other women, specifically in the painters' colony of Makartland, briefly in Japan and in the animal park in India. In India, a colossal towering organ is constructed especially for Clara.

And she played such that the wild animals stopped their roaring and looked in astonishment at the sky above. (Scheerbart 1914: 53)

At that moment, Clara's excitement is increased with the news of the arrival of colourful silks from Japan. Clara allows herself to be dressed in these fabrics and

Edgar comes to know rejection and compromise. Textiles, cloth, frivolity and sensuality momentarily take over the novel, represented by Clara's expressive music, the sumptuous Japanese silks and the eighty-five-strong female entourage sent to dress her. Simultaneously, Edgar is wrangling with engineers in Ceylon, who suggest that he consider using a textile, a wire mesh structure spread with coloured glues, in his construction to better achieve his aims. He does not accept this as a viable substitute for coloured glass. Embittered, Edgar sends a rather cynical congratulatory note, warning Clara of the uncomfortable 'curse of fame' (Scheerbart 1914: 56). Almost immediately, Clara rejects coloured clothing, rejects the possibility of equality and starts to shy away from invitations to play large concerts, setting out to find her husband and support him more fully in his architectural projects, committed to wearing grey cloth with 10 per cent white. Conceptually, this moment in the novel serves as a brief foray into Semper's theories, with feminine, relational textiles (represented by Clara) as the symbolic and structural essence of architecture. However, the power balance is quickly and tacitly redressed in favour of the status quo of patriarchy.

Ideological adaptability and plurality is a thread throughout the novel. Clara is perplexed by Edgar's seemingly inappropriate yet fixed vision for glass architecture in the polar setting of Makartland. Her clothing adapts to the conditions, thanks to a skilful seamstress who interprets the 10 per cent white to commonly include fur, suitable for the climate. Käte Bandel, a painter and close companion of Clara, takes up this topic again. She talks about how the wooden architecture that already exists in Makartland supplies both the qualities of functionalism and sensualism – noise reduction and 'coziness' (Scheerbart 1914: 33). The culturally indiscriminate nature of the principles of modernism is particularly evident during their visits to fictional locations in Japan, India and Arabia, where Clara's grey clothing is heavily criticized and subverted. In Japan, the Marquise Fi-Boh challenges Edgar about his wife's grey cloth, branding it repugnant (Scheerbart 1914: 41).

> As he entered the cabin, Herr Krug wondered more than just slightly how his wife could adjust so well to each situation. (Scheerbart 1914: 27)

Clara's behaviour throughout the novel is symbolically textile-like in its relational, matrixial qualities. She adapts well to the customs and conditions of each

The dynamic between Clara and Edgar is echoed in the relationships of modernists such as Sonia and Robert Delaunay, Anni and Josef Albers and, later, Jacqueline and Jacques Groag and Charles and Ray Eames. The female is no less of a creative leader but societally bound to the quieter, 'softer' design fields of textiles, clothing and costume often disregarding their training. Gardner Troy (2006: 15) comments on how many of the leading textile designers of the era adopted textiles as their primary discipline through necessity, as a means of developing a sense of autonomy in their relationships with their famous husbands.

> Sonia Delaunay . . . is noted by historians for her 'instinctive' feeling for colour, whereas her husband, Robert, is attributed as having formulated a colour theory. Robert Delaunay embodies the male stereotype as logical and intellectual, Sonia embodies the female stereotype as instinctive and emotional. (Buckley 1986: 238)

Whitney Chadwick, in her commentary on the Delaunays's relationship, describes how much of art history is happy to portray this relationship as 'untroubled (by) relations of dominance and subordination' (Chadwick 1993: 32).

She outlines the standard depiction of their characters within the literature, where Sonia is painted as

> [A] Russian Jewish expatriate, all warmth and generosity, quietly adjusted herself to his needs, setting aside her own career as a painter and instead devoting herself to applying his esthetic theories to the decorative arts, and the creation of a welcoming environment for the couple's many friends. (Chadwick 1993: 32)

However, Chadwick proceeds to delve deeper into an understanding of the synergy of their marriage, focusing on the concept of 'simultaneity' (a theory of colour, abstraction and expression), traditionally attributed to Robert, but which seemingly was developed in tandem and with mutable emphasis in the work of both Robert and Sonia. At the same time that Scheerbart was writing *The Gray Cloth*, Sonia Delaunay began making 'simultaneous' dresses and fabrics, arguably a key development in their joint concept which freed colour and form from the static canvas to the physical body. Chadwick quotes a poem by Blaise Cendrars written about Sonia's new work:

> colours undress you through contrast; On her dress she wears her body

This powerful statement hints at the continuing legacy of Sonia's ideas in their

Buckley's 1986 paper *Made in Patriarchy* encouraged a feminist analysis of the history of women in design and explains many of the reasons for the gendering of design disciplines, as well as the marginalization of those associated with the feminine. Andreas Huyssen (1986) takes the concept further, positioning and exposing the feminization of mass culture and its resulting denigration quite specifically at the dawn of modernist thought. David Brett (2005: 184–214) provides a detailed exploration of the subjugation of the decorative in modernist ideology and its implications to consumption and gender.

Thinking about the place of textiles in the modernist movement highlights several points of discussion. The idealism of modernism opened up the design discipline of textiles to a wider range of creative practitioners, with many artists and architects working in or with textiles, or with 'truthful' materiality in mind. However, it was still women who largely populated the discipline. If we proceed to consider the feminine aligned to the postmodern paradigm due to its relational, matrixial characteristics, and textiles as gendered in femininity, this reveals the contradiction of textiles as the ideal medium of modernism. Textiles had been appropriated by the concept of Gesamtkunstwerk and was paradoxically marginalized by it: the feminine cloaked in the masculine.

A version of this liberal feminism is illustrated when Clara commits herself to further the acceptance of colourful glass architecture and gleefully remarks how her voluntary appearance in grey, with 10 per cent white, helped her husband close a deal with a client in Cyprus (Scheerbart 1914: 77). She disregards her own persona to become more 'equal' in partnership with her husband and 'works' to develop his business.

In 2012, Leah Armstrong curated a digital resource to accompany the exhibition 'Portraits: Women Designers' at the Fashion and Textiles Museum, London. Eight out of the thirteen women designers featured in Armstrong's collection were textile designers working in post-war Britain. The images gathered by Armstrong from the photographic library of the Council of Industrial Design are products of their time, and I do not wish to become too heavily involved in visual analysis here but rather to use them as an illustration of the problematic of the gendered role of the textile designer and its effect on the status and knowledge of textile design. As Armstrong summarizes in her obvious textile design 'tools'. Behind her are lever arch folders and a set square and her demeanour in the image is awkward. Dr Marianne Straub is casually dressed, leaning forward as if listening, while fondling some fabric swatches. Shirley Craven appears to be naked in a model-like profile shot, sitting in front of her designs. Althea McNish seems to be just a stylish young woman selecting patterns for her interior decoration from a swatch book. These highly successful, prolific and pioneering designers are depicted primarily as women, with their role as a designer hidden from view, simplistically represented or intentionally misrepresented, emphasizing their femininity and/or domesticity rather than their profession.

Although writing closer to the time of their births, there are uncanny comparisons between Scheerbart's story and the relationships of other designer couples working at the later stages of modernism – for example, textile designer Hilde Pilke who changed her name to Jacqueline Groag on her marriage to architect Jacques Groag (Armstrong 2012). There are particular parallels also to Charles and Ray Eames. Neuhart and Neuhart's lengthy double volume on the Eames's (2010) makes pains to suggest that Ray Eames's credits to the commercial and creative success of the Eames Studio has been exaggerated, perpetuated publicly (but not privately) by Charles Eames himself. They state that although Ray did creatively contribute that her main role was 'first and foremost Mrs Charles Eames' (Neuhart 2010) and that she was unendingly devoted to this role, cemented by an alleged pact for no children. In the same breath Neuhart and Neuhart are less than complimentary about her personality – her incapability of making decisions and maddening unprofessionalism – and indeed, rather unnecessarily, her physique. In their biographical account of her, often drawn from personal experiences the authors having been Eames Office employees, they focus on her painstaking choices in clothing, her own and that which she selected for Charles – more parallels with *The Gray Cloth*. They mention Ray's abilities in interior design and presentation, her sensitivity to colour and form – her decorative sensibilities. In the late 1940s she created several textile designs for the Eames Office as well as magazine covers which utilized her painterly abilities. After this period, she created very little work of her own and dedicated herself to being the architect of the Eames image and reputation. Her background, which financially enabled the Eames Office existence as well as her own talents

Indeed in his review of Scheerbart's book, Victor Margolin decides that Clara's voluntary donning of the grey cloth does not come about by patriarchal coercion, and that in doing so she does not compromise her artistic power (Margolin 2003: 94). I disagree. Although it is unclear from the novel why exactly Clara makes this decision, I believe this act symbolizes societal suppression and her fear of her own power. The argument of whether women's clothing detracted from architectural design was never her own. She is 'assimilated into its protocols' and ultimately becomes its scapegoat as she negotiates the notoriety and fame her grey clothing generates. There is a clear correlation between the point at which Clara begins to voluntarily accept her grey clothing, the rejection of her own fame and her yearning for domestic life, pleading with Edgar for their extended air-bound honeymoon to come to an end. Edgar tells her that he plans to build an extension to his house at Isola Grande especially for her:

> the room is not that large and there is a harmonium in it. When you play, one hears it best in the large dining room. While playing you cannot be seen at all from the deep-set room. You can also read and write there. You will like it.

She expresses her desire for it to be coloured in grey tones:

> 'Oh' shouted Frau Clara, 'that is indeed wonderful'. (Scheerbart 1914: 96)

> You cannot imagine . . .how much I long for quiet domesticity and how happy I am about my gray room in which my harmonium is placed. Yes! (Scheerbart 1914: 100)

Here again, we can draw parallels between Sonia Delaunay's real life and Clara's fictional one. At the height of Sonia's commercial success and Robert's downturn, Sonia talks of how 'success literally assailed me', 'I was capable of being a woman manager, but I had other purposes in life' (Delaunay n.d. in Chadwick 1993: 47). It was at the point when the worldwide recession affected sales of her work that the tables turned again and it was once again Robert's moment in the light.

I feel that Clara decides to adopt the grey cloth voluntarily as a way of settling rumours, negating speculation and to show acceptance of her marital status, situation and domestic life. Scheerbart tells us quite directly that Clara starts to turn away from her music. Once installed in Isola Grande, Clara is compelled to spend her time not in the grey room but in an emerald room, shining with amethyst ornament, housing orchids which she meticulously cares for under by Iris Marion Young in her interpretation of the writing of Luce Irigaray and Simone de Beauvoir:

> To fix and keep hold of his identity, man makes a house, put things in it, and confines there his woman who reflects his identity to him. The price she pays for supporting his subjectivity, however, is dereliction, having no self of her own. (Young 1990: 124)

I propose that *The Gray Cloth* provides a metaphor for the paradox of textiles in the modernist design context. Clara's narrative epitomizes the subjugation of textile design practices into modernist ideology. This story prompts a consideration of the disciplinary entities of design and their role in the development of design research and, consequentially, design history. It instantiates the dichotomy of architectonic and textilic practices (Ingold 2010). Hierarchies of accepted knowledge production established through a hylomorphic ontology and historically gendered-making practices collaborate to suppress varied approaches and understandings of design. This suppression persists and therefore requires a pluralist, intersectional feminist critique to highlight abandoned or influenced contributions to design history and research.

# 8

# The gendered textile design discipline

## Disciplinarity

A 'discipline', in the religious rather than academic sense, is a phenomenon that is simultaneously a collective and a dispersion. A 'discipline' requires disciples; individuals who feel drawn to a particular set of teachings tacitly learn and adopt the rules and rituals associated with the discipline allowing them to guide their thoughts and behaviours. Disciples follow and embrace the teachings, which may be explicit and written down or implicitly communicated. They will take comfort in knowing they share their fundamental beliefs, thoughts and behaviours with others. Essentially the disciple has a tacit relationship with the discipline, which is both internal and personal and external in relation to other disciples across time and location:

> [A] heuristic vision which is accepted for the sake of its unresolvable tension. It is like an obsession with a problem known to be insoluble, which yet, unswervingly, the heuristic commands; 'Look at the unknown!' Christianity sedulously fosters, and in a sense permanently satisfies, man's craving for mental dissatisfaction by offering him the comfort of a crucified God. (Polanyi 1958: 212)

Using Polanyi's religious analogy for man's craving for mental dissatisfaction and applying it to the shared knowledge and purpose of designers allows us to reconsider the notion of the design 'discipline'. It helps to explain and describe the collective and permanent mental dissatisfaction that drives individuals who call themselves 'designers'. There is a shared vision of an all-encompassing unsolvable problem: a compelling intellectual passion, easily triggered.

Once we have learned to do something in a certain way, we will tend to do that thing the same way forever, or until a 'better' way presents itself (and sometimes, not even then). In this way, we will tend to not try other ways to do a thing because we have learned one way of doing it.

Design has been traditionally categorized into disciplines, which include many sub-disciplines that become specialisms for specific designers: for instance, fashion design includes specialists in knitwear, tailoring and underwear, among others. The boundaries between disciplines are becoming less clear, with many polymath designers producing a range of successful design outcomes. For example, Hella Jongerius's signature style has been incorporated into designs for furniture, ceramics, lighting and footwear. This approach supports the notion that the design process is a consistent and transferable practice or procedure, which can be applied with relevance and success in all fields of design.

Any 'model' of the design process, with no specificity in regard to specialism, separates the design process from the particular making, manufacturing processes and techniques that are integral to designing. It assumes that the specialist knowledge required to design different kinds of objects effectively has little or no bearing on how a designer might approach designing in the first place. When making is removed from the process for the sake of constructing a generalized model, it may not adequately cover the range of versions of the design process that will be experienced by designers working in all sectors of the field. For an area such as textile design, one that reaches into craft and applied arts, such a model is problematic. If, however, we accept that the procedures associated with designing are transferable and universally intrinsic, then we must also ask why most designers specialize within one area or sub-discipline of design.

Wang and Ilhan (2009: 5) 'propose a sociological distinctiveness to the design professions which is really their key distinguishing signature'. They oppose the notion that individual design professions hold specific knowledge and that there are social, historical and market-led reasons for this concept being maintained in academic writing. They describe a 'sociological wrapping' around the 'creative act' and proceed in their investigation by questioning what a profession is; they do not assume that different design professions possess a specific knowledge, but rather that they are all centred round the creative act. They present this as second the sociological wrapping of disciplines or professions. Wang and Ilhan advise that in order to define a design profession one must decipher what it does '(with any general knowledge that assists in the creative act) in a sociological process of defining itself to the larger culture' (Wang and Ilhan 2009: 7). The authors use architecture, interior design and industrial design as examples of three professions at different stages of defining a professional identity. They consider that, of the three, industrial design is the 'least professionalized by sociological standards'. This statement seems to be based on the number of US designers subscribing to membership of professional organizations. They argue that although all three professions vary in regard to organized and structured professional standards, what they share is the fact that the knowledge they possess is not 'domain-specific'. Wang and Ilhan conclude by questioning the difference between 'discipline' and 'profession', referencing an online discussion topic started by Ken Friedman on the subject in 2007. Wang and Ilhan state regularly in their paper that the ideas they propose are counter to the common discourse, and that they challenge concepts developed by leading academics in the field of design research.

The discipline or profession of textiles has not been as rigorously professionalized as areas such as architecture but there are several accounts exploring and purporting to explore the specificities of textile knowledge, in both design literature and material culture studies. As such, it remains a worthwhile activity to find a location for textiles knowledge in the wider field of design precisely because it may yield new insights into the creative act for textile designers and/or designers in general. The notion of 'sociological wrapping' is of importance and one which, whether in agreement with Wang and Ilhan's proposals against domain-specific knowledge or not, is something that many in the field of design may readily recognize.

Textile design appears to attract a broad range of 'disciples'. As shown in Figure 1, the term 'textile practitioner' can at once describe students, artists, craftspeople, hobbyists and designers of various levels of expertise, approaches and experience, all with markedly different approaches to following and embracing the 'teachings' of the discipline. Textile design encompasses teachings from the broader disciplines of design, art and craft, indicating that textile design disciples have formed a tacit understanding of a specific blend discipline has particular protocols for presenting design ideas (Moxey 2000) that are not shared with any other sub-discipline of design, while even commonly used systems for recording design thinking and process, such as sketchbooks, will be used in subtly differing ways. It would be extraneous for me here to provide a potted history of the development of the textile design discipline or the textile design industry, and in any case this has been the concern of many design and industrial historians. Here I focus on the idiosyncrasies of the textile design discipline and the specific characteristics of textile designers, asking what behaviours or methods they share which combine to define textile knowledge and the textile design discipline? What Wang and Ilhan propose invites me to consider the sociological wrapping of textile design. How has the discipline developed, and how is it perceived? How does it operate and present itself? As Buckley (1986) implies, textile design has been (and is) sociologically gendered (also see Mesh Two and the preceding chapter). The gendered wrapping of textile design and its delay in professionalizing itself has affected its ability to have an impact on the non-domain-specific knowledge that Wang and Ilhan propose. This is emphasized in the way I have used the persona of Clara Krug in Paul Scheerbart's novel *The Gray Cloth* as a representation of textiles as an entity, incorporating yet shifting between the nexus of the textile designer, the textile discipline, the textile design process and the textile design as embodied outcome. I shall call this entity Textiles (with a capital T). I wish to push these characterizations into conceptualizations of textile design practice.

## The textile entity

I am a fresh graduate and prize winner, sitting in my own stand, one of hundreds, at an event that was then called 'Indigo' which took place at the Première Vision trade fair in Paris in 2001. I was surrounded by the varied textile design samples I had produced as a student, pinned to the wall behind me and laid out on the table in front, my name emblazoned across the top of the stand. Trade show visitors nonchalantly walked past or came for an idle rifle through the mounted samples: I could only find out who they were if I caught a glimpse of their name badge. Some people came and spoke with me, introducing themselves as fashion to sell my work. I did sell a few pieces, and many people seemed interested in my work, but soon realized that what I was offering in terms of textile design was not appropriate for that forum. I felt quite exposed, misled and misunderstood after this experience. Why had I been invited to show and sell my work there? Had I not sold it well enough? Should I have done something differently? How could I do better next time? I realized that I would be nothing if I did not please these people. I embodied my textile designs; they were full of my creativity. At the time of designing and making them I did not think about whom I would sell them to. I was concerned with the process and developing creative outcomes, but my design discipline required me to 'put it on show'.

There is an interesting dynamic between the role of the textile designer as artistic, creative and skilled and their requirement to produce work that others will enjoy and pay for. They have independency and licence in their creative endeavours, but the outcomes of their activity are destined for a supporting role in another designed product.

I progress here with the notion of textiles as an entity, gendered through social constructs as feminine, though the discipline naturally encompasses designers of all genders. The textile entity's attributes, skills and persona as a commodity prompts parallels in my mind with the life of a geisha. A muted female, highly skilled and committed to the cultivation of those skills, but regarded more simply for the pleasure and beauty their skills provide and resigned to her requirement to trade on her skills. The process by which a textile design for sale was created was of little importance, but it should be viable and must always be 'beautiful'. How it functions, be it in a classic woven form or incorporating innovative smart systems or new materials, is often of secondary importance to its decorative sensibilities. If it doesn't excel on both counts, it does succeed.

Textiles is decorative and female. Textiles must use all its performative and sublimely seductive characteristics in order to communicate possible applications to potential partners and patrons in a world which is hidden. Partners and patrons are courted, flattered and pleasured, ritually and continuously. Textiles enigmatically seduces the senses with its artistry, in a modest and submissive way. Textiles surrenders itself, allowing the partner or patron to momentarily own it.

Textiles is a geisha.

and design. A geisha must master several artistic practices, such as dance or music, and develop her ability to a high level, but the development of these skills is just an element of her entity that must ultimately express modesty and stylized traditional/historicized/cultural notions of beauty. The development of her skill is boundaried by the transaction that occurs which commissions their performance. The appearance of a geisha is highly ornate and decorated, excessively feminine, using motifs and symbols in hair and make-up to highlight this. The vast quantity of rich fabrics that their bodies are swaddled in is all part of the performance. Lesley Downer describes Koito, a geisha, as she dresses for work:

> She had become a compilation of markers of femininity – woman embodied. As she put on her make-up, her persona too began to change. She was stepping into the role, like an actor does, whereas she had been down to earth and straightforward, she became coquettish, speaking in a coy girly voice . . . . A geisha has to be expert at choosing the right kimono for the right season and the occasion. (Downer 2006: 236)

Viewing textiles-as-entity-as-geisha, applying Downer's quote, illustrates the acceptance of a subjugated (female) role as described by the textile designers. A geisha's persona is consumed by the textiles and the make-up it is swathed in, yet is indelibly marked by it. Textile designers are anonymous, yet have a distinct handwriting they are valued for, and their ability to produce designs that are just 'right' for the 'mood' or season marks their commercial success.

Once hired by a patron, a geisha's primary role is to flatter, cosset, listen, entertain and amuse them, all against an implicit backdrop of a sexual encounter: the promise of pleasure. She serves drinks, performs dances and promises the potential of pleasure. She surrenders her subjectivity to her encounter with the patron in return for his enjoyment and fulfilment. Her interior world is concealed and unspoken. Each geisha develops her own approach to this given role, which she must adapt for each patron, but the goal of providing a promise of pleasure for financial return is the overarching goal. Textile designers provide what is needed. When the brief is known in advance, they must design something that speaks of that sensation. When it is unknown, they must be able to make judgements on global aesthetic concerns and translate this into textiles, trying all those feminine characteristics embodied by the geisha: modesty, sensuality, decoration, beauty, intrigue and availability.

If you visit a textile trade show, you are likely to see the typical scenario of a textile designer's sales pitch (the 'daft situation' as a famous textile designer once called it). The textile designer (or textile studio agent) is standing up behind a table in the studio's stand (see Figure 2). Two or three people (fashion designers, interior designers, buyers, perhaps) are seated on the other side. The textile designer slowly but swiftly presents sample after sample to the seated people whose gaze is fixed steadily on the numerous beautiful and skilful designs that are moving quickly in front of their eyes. Occasionally, one of the pair reaches out to touch a sample or puts it to one side for further consideration. They know what they are looking for (they think), or at least they will know when they find it. They might make a purchase or they might walk away. The seated trio comment among themselves; the textile designer usually maintains silence while they look (Figure 2).

In this situation, textiles-as-entity is rendered mute. Judged solely on appearance, how it elicits sensation. This state is curiously liminal. The textile swatch/sample is a designed object, but it has not yet fulfilled its role. It seeks a transformation into something else, assimilation into something else, beyond just being a textile. The seated pair in the scenario above might purchase one or two samples to be developed into their fashion range. At the point of sale, most often there will be no indication of how the textile will be applied. Even

if purchased or commissioned, a textile design may go no further than the boardroom table. And what of the textile samples that are dismissed, those that are never purchased? These fully worked examples of design, these 'samples', do not achieve any transformation. They are consigned to the archive, perhaps to be retrieved and reworked when the moment 'feels' right again.

Textiles is considered simple and uncomplicated not forthcoming or interested in articulating what makes it special or unique. Its muteness has impeded its relationship with other areas of design. Textiles may be specifically chosen or even commissioned but equally may never be sold or be put into production, leaving its potential unrealized. Textiles is on the shelf. Textiles needs a suitor.

Textiles is a maiden aunt.

The notion that a designer will produce a large quantity of fully worked designs for an unknown brief, only for a fraction of them to be purchased or put into production, is unique to textile design. It occurs for both textile design studios as well as designers working 'in house' for a large company. While commenting on this 'daft situation' there is a sense it also often affords textile designers a creative autonomy. Textile designers are accepting of this status quo: perhaps it allows them the opportunity to explore a wide range of designs and processes. Textiles in sample form, when in exhibitions or displayed for commercial sales are often better understood in these circumstances when incorporated into a mock product – often seen at textile trade shows as 'garment fronts'. Friedman (2003: 513–14) offers a viewpoint which contextualizes this situation in design theory:

> On occasion, the intuitive practice of design produces unpredictable desirable results that can be seized retrospectively as the useable result of muddling through. Far more often, however, muddling through produces failures of two kinds. The first kind of failure involves proposals that fail in the early stages of conception or development. This is a good time for failure, since failure in conception or development eliminates potentially wasteful efforts. The second kind of failure involves completed attempts at solutions in which the designers believe that they have solved the problem even though they have not done so. This is far more costly in every sense. One of the central aspects of this kind of failure is the fact that some designers never learn that they have actually failed to meet client needs, customer needs, or end-user needs. This is because designers often end their involvement with the project before the failures arise and the clients of most failures do not return to the original designer for repair work.

'failures', which certainly frames this viewpoint. Nonetheless, the second thing it highlights is the very nature of the 'daft situation'; the production of all these 'possible' design solutions is costly and wasteful in terms of time and materials for the designer or company. The third point it captures is the sheltered position this situation creates for the designer. For textile designers, selling designs to other designers at the first level of consumption (Figure 1), their position is quite unique, their relationship with the ultimate end user can be distant, yet the impact of their work is crucial. Exposed is a deeply problematic, irrational system and unsustainable trading model. Despite this continuing as the mainstream vehicle for textile design commerce, recent and ongoing research into circular design models is challenging this in the face of the need for sustainable business models (Goldsworthy and Earley 2018; Vuletich 2015).

In relating textiles to the stereotypical maiden aunt, it exposes the often taciturn nature of the textile design discipline, uninterested in participating in the wider discourse of design research and naïve to what it might contribute. Textiles is the quiet girl sitting in the back row. 'Maiden aunt' is a somewhat quainter and kinder label for a woman who could equally be called a 'spinster'. A spinster, a female spinner of thread or a female who remains unmarried beyond the normal age, emphasizes the often negative socially constructed feminine gendering of textile practice. The maiden aunt/spinster metaphor also speaks of the unfulfilled textile design sample/swatch, complete and beautiful but consigned to the shelf and never put into production. These forgotten 'virgins' of textile design practice invite a closer investigation into the historical, social and economic factors that affected the development of trading and other business systems in commercial textile design and other related industries. In other words, how did the 'daft situation' described above come to be common practice, when models of commissioning, pitching or licensing for design work might be a more appropriate system?

The textile design that is put into production and applied to a garment or a sofa – how can this scenario be conceptualized? In a sense it undergoes an adverse state change from designed object to component or raw material for the purposes of being applied within a subsequent designed product. It allows a new product to come into being. The presence of the textile design may be obvious and integral to the new product.

Textiles enables other designed products to come into existence. It is a fertile

Textiles is a mother.

It is no new concept to find parallels with material and motherhood; they are etymologically linked. What I seek to do in coming to this metaphor is to consider how it affects our conception of the design process. Textile designs become raw materials or components for other types of designers, putting a level between textiles and wood, plastic and animal skin (all of which can be surface-designed in the manner of a textile, too, but nonetheless are natural or engineered substances). It reminds me of a quote from William Morris, discussing decoration and ornamentation:

> ... in many or most cases we have got so used to this ornament that we look upon it as if had grown of itself, and note it of no more than mosses on the dry sticks with which we light our fires. (Morris 1877)

This state change places textiles in the peculiar position of being a designed object that comes first, allowing others to come into being but is marginalized. The feminine entity of 'textiles' brings other designed objects into existence by communicating potential and translating pleasure at the same time as being marginalized and ignored. The perception of textile design as a raw material, seen as natural, may actually speak of the cultural significance and sensorial power of textiles. Textiles are surrendered to the subsequent product. But what if we were to envisage this situation as a version of Ettinger's metramorphosis, in a trans-subjective matrixial encounter, with textiles-as-mother where each participant are partners-in-difference, their experiences changed and linked? This places textiles in a synergistic relationship.

By characterizing textiles as an entity aligned with the social construct of the feminine, I have incited three contentious metaphors. Metaphor, of course, is often used a key device for the marginalization, subjugation and trivialization of women and their lives, and feminists have both challenged and utilized metaphor as a means of emphasizing their argument.

Translations

You show me the poems of some woman my age, or younger,
translated from your language
Certain words occur: enemy, oven, sorrow
enough to let me know she's a woman of my time

worn it like lead on our ankles
watched it through binoculars as if
it were a helicopter
bringing food to our famine
or the satellite of a hostile power

I begin to see that woman doing things:
stirring rice
ironing a skirt
typing a manuscript till dawn

trying to make a call
from a phonebooth

The phone rings endlessly
in a man's bedroom
she hears him telling someone else
Never mind. She'll get tired.
hears him telling her story to her sister

who becomes her enemy
and will in her own way
light her own way to sorrow
ignorant of the fact this way of grief
is shared, unnecessary
and political

In its first few lines, *Translations*, by poet Adrienne Rich (1972), indicates the endurance of metaphors in shaping and limiting female lives. The line I find particularly powerful is '. . . hears him telling her story to her sister'. It captures the crucial importance of narrative feminist qualitative research methodologies as well as the requirement of a feminist critique of design research. Rich's metaphors of the female obsession with love as gardening and baking initially seem steeped in the domestic, but this is quickly countered by the inference of a military context: women's passions held hostage. This sudden reframing of the metaphor at this point in the poem positions women not as cosy housewives but as political prisoners of conceptual correspondences' (Lakoff 1993: 207). In the way that I have utilized metaphor, I have conceptually mapped the characteristics of textiles and femininity onto one another, identifying those 'correspondences' within the context of design.

In using the archetypes of geisha, spinster and mother, I do not wish to communicate a reciprocation of these patriarchal labels but point to how the textiles entity has both tacitly subscribed and been held to these roles. The labels of geisha, mother and maiden aunt or spinster have some correlation with notions of the neopaganist concept of the 'triple goddess' of maiden, mother and crone, as well as Jungian archetypes, though I do not want to present them in this way. The specificity of the labels chosen enact the feminist activity of 'naming' and reclaiming terms so that alternative scenarios are provided. Delving into the geisha, spinster and mother metaphors for textiles allows a feminist reading of its position in the design hierarchy and how its character as an entity, embodied in the nexus of the textile design, the textile design process, the textile industry and the textile designer, has contributed to its taciturnity in relation to design research.

Exposing these metaphors of the entity of textile design appears to play to gender binarisms, forgoing concepts of the post-gender cyborg (Haraway 2006) of feminist technoscience. Indeed, in the following chapter Marion Lean extends the metaphoric archetypes through her applied research into innovative textiles. The Mother, the Father, the Spinster, the Sportsperson, the Geisha and the Soldier serve here as narrative mechanisms to expose the need to challenge the phallogocentrism of theories of design research and I explore Ettinger's matrixiality as a framework for this. Daniela Rosner (2018) uses the backdrop of feminist technoscience to develop her critical fabulations of and as design. Kathrin Thiele (2014) provides a reading of differentiation and diffraction in the work of posthumanist scholars Karen Barad, Donna Haraway and Vicki Kirby as a lens for the notion of difference in the work of Bracha Ettinger. Thiele (2014: 208) calls this 'diffracting (new) feminist materialisms with matrixiality'. Thiele underlines that Ettinger's feminine metaphoracity is not to be taken as any biological binarism or prioritization of motherhood or pregnancy but instead matrixiality is an 'apparatus for conductible affectivity, which gives voice to the affected body-psyche co-emerging with the other and the world' (Pollock of co-emergence. It provides proof in point that the thinking used in the process of making textilic structures is innately relational and set in a co-emergent encounter with their context. Thiele attempts to reconcile the approaches from the feminist theorists she explores and suggests an ethos where it is recognized that '"we" are always/already entangled with-in everything' (Thiele 2014: 213). 'We' does not point to fixed embodied subjectivities but a woven textile/texture subjective 'encounter-event' (Ettinger 2006a).

Applying the matrixial framework to the archetypes recognizes and implicates the social constructs of the Mother, Spinster and Geisha archetypes of textiles in their own weaving and in the weaving of the concept of the textile design discipline and thus the weaving of theories of design. This entangled agency means 'we' (as above) are already in design research but the ethos of diffraction that Thiele discusses has not been activated within the development of design research.

> With diffraction – both as concept and as apparatus via which we envision difference differently – we witness a change in attitude: an opening up of the whole engagement with difference(s) and differentiality as 'a mapping of interference, not of replication, reflection or reproduction.' (Thiele quoting Haraway 2014: 204)

# 9

# Taking on textile thinking

Marion Lean

In my final degree year of textile design at Duncan of Jordanstone College of Art in 2011, fellow students perfected their repeat floral prints, applied for internships at Timorous Beasties, pulled all-nighters in the knit room and pulled hair in the queue for the laser cutter. I had begun to think about problems which were outside of the print room. I felt burdened by a high level of practical textile design ability (print) but minimal ideas of how to apply this to social challenges. I set myself a design challenge to address health awareness, in particular smoking, through textile design.

My final undergraduate collection *Alter Mind, Trigger Behaviour* used the textile technique 'devoré' (from French, literally to devour, also known as burn out) to represent the slow but deadly deterioration of the body in response to smoking. Conceptualizing the body as material, the destructive breakdown of the body through smoking, was mimicked by deterioration of fabric. Though a beautiful and well-produced collection of prints and fabric manipulation, my passion lay not in the finished material outcome but in the new information I'd collected about issues in other fields (public health, social science, activism), now embedded in a textile collection. In a 2011 blog post I described my work as 'embracing and contesting perceived textile design thinking methodology'. A drive which was misunderstood/confused by attendees at New Designers graduate design exhibition who were not expecting to be finding delicate bodysuits with blacked-out lungs.

As friends went off to design internships at trend forecasting agencies and high-street chain head offices, I joined the MA in critical practice at Goldsmiths, University of London. The intention was to establish a means to apply my (art) textiles department. Many years on, I might have handled that conversation differently, but being a newly arrived Scot in London I thought I best *ca canny*.

During my MA, I found ways that I could apply my textile knowledge in the briefs set. Through a textiles lens (expanded on later in Lean 2020), yet not limited to the textile medium, I developed new ideas, tried new technologies and collaborated with designers from a range of disciplines, including interaction design, branding and architecture, to create outputs including films, projection mapping and public installation. The themes I explored included lack of tangibility in online social-media relationships, perception of the body and time travel. Textile thinking in this experience led to projects which though textile oriented were ultimately undisciplined, new and exciting. This work led to professional experience developing wearable technology that connects people across continents using haptic feedback. Observations about tactile sensibility developed into my hunch that the discipline of textiles which centres around the sense of touch has the potential to critique the practices of technology and data, which are typically screen-based, untouchable and immaterial.

I enrolled for a practice-based PhD at the Royal College of Art (RCA) in 2016, compelled to return to my interests surrounding body and health messaging, this time bringing experience in Internet of Things (IOT), wearable technology and consumer electronics. I aimed to use textile thinking to address body representation and experience using technology such as sensors, fitness trackers and so forth. To begin with I worried I wasn't a 'real' textile designer; I didn't create metres of beautiful fabric or collaborate with product and fashion designers or create new materials. During my master's course, my early textile training was complimented by opportunities to learn from others through collaboration outside of the textile design discipline and the development of my design methodology which is motivated by emerging concerns and criticisms about technologies. In my varied creative practice, whether developing an installation or in my facilitation of others, I not only bring an interest in the material object but additionally in bringing people together in a physical space to have an experience and together create an atmosphere to create and debate ideas. Rather than limiting my approach to developing physical textile and material outcomes I was keen to explore how textile thinking approaches applied in design research could lead to insights and innovation which may be themes, collaborating, asking questions, engaging others and experimenting with technology to explore new mediums and dimensions for design. *The Tacit-Turn: Textile Design in Design Research* (Igoe 2010) and *In Textasis: Matrixial Narratives of Textile Design* (Igoe 2013) became key reading for understanding examples of textile thinking. Igoe's work aimed to widen the scope of the field of textiles so that it might be understood as design and freed from the boundaries of 'craft' labelling. However, I felt there were some areas that needed additions if it was to align with my experience of design and thinking in textiles. In particular within atypical environments outside the studio, using 'materials' as a loose term encompassing people, data, insights and outcomes which could be described as experiences and experiments rather than samples or swatches.

I began to develop a series of hypotheses to 'take on' textile thinking – experiments which might identify and test the concept of textile thinking. The aim being to expand our epistemological understanding of textile thinking and reveal the potential impact of textile design practice and research applied in wider multidisciplinary engagements.

Igoe's work (2013 and this volume) aims to reveal the embodied, tacit nature of textile cognition, argues for recognition of intricate, enigmatic, non-linear design methods and for these practices to be integrated into and acknowledged in design research. The tacit knowledge and intuition embedded in the thinking and making of textile practice methodologies have rarely been documented. For textile practitioners, regularly collaborating in other fields means they often work in non-linear ways, to build sensitivities, nuances and understandings of new fields and develop tacit knowledge through interdisciplinary working. From clothing to cars, the role of the textile designer is integrated across an expansive range of industries. However, textiles' input is often shrouded by the other disciplines or seen as mere decoration, regarded as an addition instead of recognizing textiles' 'designerly' contribution to the whole. More recently, textile design-led approaches which enable others by facilitating interaction and engagement are being explored in different settings and contexts. Use of textile design-like activities in projects addressing loneliness (Nevay 2017) and supporting those living with dementia (Robertson 2019) show how textile thinking functioning outside of the textiles domain can produce or contribute to knowledge generation. Researchers in the area of textiles and sustainability, in particular textile recycling (Hall and Earley valued form and process of knowledge generation in design still struggles to be acknowledged; this has been noted by Ballie (2014; Philpott and Kane (2013, 2016) and Valentine et al. (2017).

Igoe identifies key characteristics of the textile design process and textile thinking, both tacit and explicit, and places them within the context of design research. Textiles is presented as a collective 'entity' that draws together designers, objects and processes and is given three identities as mother, geisha and spinster. She uses metaphor in labelling to communicate and decipher intangible or inherent understandings held within the disciplinary field of textiles. The three entities adequately and artfully cover the scope of decorative aesthetics in textile design practice. The 'Mother', often behind the scenes, or in the synergies, resonates with Igoe's interview findings with textile designers describing their experiential relationships with industry – for example, developing textile designs for fashion products. The 'Geisha' represents textiles' aesthetic qualities performing to engage and enhance experience. The 'Spinster', however, is curious and pushes boundaries.

I believe that the three entities described by Igoe are at risk of further pigeonholing a mystical 'textiley' nature of practice and that they should be expanded into other roles to support emerging textile practices. I explore here additional attributes which could represent the emerging role of textile designers within multidisciplinary working environments in particular where collaboration with technologies is concerned.

In order to explore a 'new' or expanded version of textile thinking for these emerging fields I named additional 'entities' that I identified through my own research – textile thinking behaviours which are based on interaction, decision-making and resilience. I employed Igoe's entities in two experiments. First, in Testing Textile Thinking 1, as a tool for analysis, looking at where textile thinking could be identified in the development of smart textile prototypes, a key field of growth for textile practice. And second, in Testing Textile Thinking 2, as an interactive data collection tool where designers from all disciplines could explore textile thinking aspects in their own practices.

# Testing Textile Thinking 1

and Mass Customisation (ITMC). Responding to the fact that smart textiles and 'wearable intelligence' are facing integration and expansion into other disciplinary fields and marketplaces, the event invites designers and researchers to present recent prototypes as an indication of current research in this space. Using the salon as a selection of the most up-to-date examples, I examined the objective and subjective attributes of a range of smart textiles and wearable technology innovations with applications in personal use for health and well-being, environment, construction and transport. After an initial survey, it was clear that Igoe's original 'entities' could not sufficiently cater for all the textile technology collaborations on show at the event. This three-part entity concept represents the role of the textile designer in design agendas where empathy, emotion and expressivity are collectively considered. However, when it is applied to design of wearable technologies, or in a smart textile context, this concept tended to miss some qualities, in particular, attributes which link to current technological applications and collaborative methodologies, so I added further attributes.

The exhibition at the salon featured twenty-nine exhibitors from academic research labs, independent research centres and small business owners in Europe, the United States and North Africa. Prototypes and demonstrations were exhibited as working samples or systems and each exhibitor also gave a short introductory presentation. Some of the prototypes were created in order to showcase a technology. Others were samples of materials without application, at an early stage or looking for collaborative partners to develop the work further. The event was an opportunity to meet with researchers in the fields of materials and smart materials to understand the processes and challenges of the research stage and gain perspective into the trajectories of collaboration involved in applied research and market opportunities. The prototypes and short descriptions were collated in a catalogue which was used to support my analysis. I reviewed aspects of the development processes for smart materials and products displayed and created an analysis tool to input 'data' from each exhibited prototype. The tool was a form with three categories to identify types of projects:

- Object – including material, system and sensors used
- Innovation – including information about the team, the collaboration methods, funding drivers, the destined industry and if the innovation was

Of the twenty-nine exhibits, most of the prototypes were designed for personal use (sixteen) or for use on the body, with environment (nine) and portable (four) applications the remaining. The potential industries served by the range of smart textile prototypes featured were health/sport/well-being (sixteen), outdoor/construction (three), automotive (two) and clothing/safety/art (eight). The majority of the examples took the form of a technical inquiry (twelve), alongside materials inquiry (ten) and social and design-led inquiry (five). Particular evidence of textile thinking present in the examples included consideration of physical intimacy; need to be close to the body/skin, supportive; the use of traditional construction techniques; and to provide 'alternative readings of a situation' such as metaphor. Other significant additional attributes in the prototypes included being strong, durable or resilient – concerned with measurement and quantifying and the role of the textile itself as a way of disguising technology.

The results showed that of the projects analysed, four aligned solely with the characteristics of the original textile entities and one used solely additional or 'new' textile thinking characteristics as described earlier. The remaining twenty-four examples showed a balanced mixture of characteristics.

In Figure 3, I outline Igoe's classification of textiles as three entities and show the additional attributes evident in the emerging field of smart textiles and wearable technologies. I classified these as Sportsperson, Soldier and Father to encompass 'new' textile thinking characteristics.

The focus of my investigation in Testing Textile Thinking 1 was not solely on 'textile' outcomes or objects but in areas where textile designers and researchers have contributed to social or technological solutions where the outcome is not easily identifiable as textiles, such as service design ideation in the design of a wearable technology product. For example, Martijn ten Bhömer (2016) used models to explore experience in his study of the use of prototypes for 'embodied sense making'. Physical objects helped stakeholders develop ideas about immaterial concepts such as services. Ten Bhömer found that physical prototypes could be used at the design meeting stage to imagine the product in use, to illustrate the product in relation to the body and to propose intangible design features and smart textile services, including digital functionality or sound.

| TEXTILE ENTITIES | | |
|---|---|---|
| Mother | Geisha | Spinster |
| Enable other objects to come into existence/becoming<br><br>Invites (and requires) partners to participate in realizing new creations<br><br>Relates, adapts<br><br>Communicates<br><br>Gives<br><br>Physical | Indigenous social perspective provides alternative readings of a situation (metaphor)<br><br>Performative<br><br>Decorative<br><br>Seductive<br><br>Exquisite<br><br>Patron receives a particular level of control over the behaviour<br><br>(Potential of) sensory pleasure | Simple, uncomplicated<br><br>Muteness, inability to forge relationships<br><br>Overlooked by those looking only for beauty<br><br>Academic<br><br>Pursues own interests (curious) |

| NEW TEXTILE THINKING ENTITIES | | |
|---|---|---|
| Sportsperson | Soldier | Father |
| Measurement, quantify<br><br>Competitive<br><br>Communication<br><br>Dedication, motivation, focus<br><br>Strength<br><br>Discipline, commitment<br><br>Confidence, optimist | Fighting, courage, strong, Endurance<br><br>Functional<br><br>Teamwork, loyalty<br><br>Decisiveness, judgement, initiative<br><br>Knowledge, awareness<br><br>Selfless service | Provider<br><br>Leader, verbally expressive (compared to Mother seen as less visible)<br><br>To be seen, role model<br><br>Dependable<br><br>Immediate<br><br>Resilient<br><br>Protector<br><br>Teacher<br><br>Disciplinarian |

**Figure 3** Expanded textile thinking entities (adapted from Lean 2017/2020).

materials. The addition of the further three entities was intended to incorporate functional aspects of a designed textile prototype as a way of studying an object using a specific lens and enabled a guided interrogation. The Mother and the Father are the same but different. The textile designer-facilitator does not solely contribute to aesthetics yet performs all the tasks required of her, interlacing

## Testing Textile Thinking 2

To test the characteristics of the entities in Figure 3 and to see if they feature in other fields of practice, I created an interactive exhibit as a platform for others to describe their practice based on the key characteristics. In 2018, during an interim 'Work in Progress' student show at the RCA, visitors were invited to map the characteristics of their practice using the list of descriptions and icons shown in Figure 4.

The icons and descriptions of characteristics (Figure 4) were displayed on a sandwich board in the form of a spectrum–like clock face (Figure 5). The tool was designed so that visitors could engage with the characteristics by first reading the description to learn what each entailed and then choosing on a scale from 1 (a little) to 5 (a lot) how much they felt each characteristic featured in their own practice. Numbered nails (1–5) and coloured builder's line allowed exhibition visitors to trace out aspects of their practice. Visitors chose a coloured line according to their identified practice – designer, non-designer or textile designer. Their responses created patterns and the visitors interacted with an exhibition piece to create a data 'materialisation' (Lean 2020) in a visual, tactile and tangibly sociable way. The results showed that the textile thinking characteristics I'd illustrated and arranged in numbered scale (1–5 for how relevant each characteristic was) could be used to describe elements of practice by both textile designers and other designers. This showed how textile thinking characteristics could be used to analyse design practice and outcomes. This exercise enabled dialogue between the participants and myself about the concept of textile thinking; how textile designers think and the characteristics

| Enabling, | Seduce, | Curiosity, | Measurement, | Discipline, | To be seen, |
|---|---|---|---|---|---|
| inviting others, | disguise, | independent | dedication, | decisiveness, | role model, |
| support, | metaphor, | thinking, | motivation, | judgement | dependable, |
| relates, | sensory | Simple, | focus, | initiative, | immediate |
| adapts | pleasure | uncomplicated | confidence, | knowledge, | Resilient |
| communicates | | | optimist | awareness | |

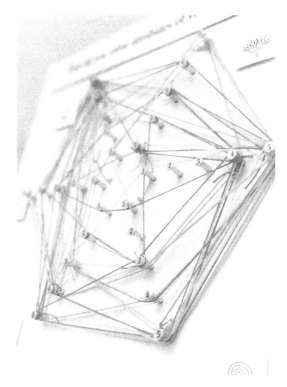

**Figure 5** Textile thinking interactive exhibit at the Royal College of Art, London, UK (2018).

of that practice; and initiated discussions on the transferability of textile approaches in other domains. By applying human, relational characteristics to activities and outcomes of design practice, data in the form of designed objects and individual behaviours and design decisions were analysed using metaphors of human relations, emotions and entities (Mother, Geisha, Spinster, Sportsperson, Soldier, Father). Observations from these experiments suggested potential for the expansion of the repertoire of textile design approaches and activities particularly with regard to technology-oriented textile outcomes but also in some design activities that do not produce a 'traditional' textile (material) outcome.

## Textile thinking in practice

has focused in particular on the use of material practices as tools for research but where the 'final' outcome may well be quite 'immaterial', for example, the design of a service, system or interaction. In this, I developed a formal set of qualities which are presented as a visual methodology map for textile thinking as a research practice (Lean 2020). This map as a practice-based research contribution is useful for textile design researchers as a tool to aid collaboration in multidisciplinary settings – for example, to communicate one's approach. This is also relevant to textile design practitioners and researchers who can use this as a framework to identify and find value in aspects of their existing practices. I continue to carry out design activities and lead research encounters which, while previously could be seen as atypical for textile design, can now be identified, against the work of others *as* textile design which crosses boundaries, fosters relationships and enables new ways of designing in research.

Further to this I propose seven criteria for textile design research: applying tacit knowledge; affect and being in the synergies; experimenting with materialities; problem setting; engaging technology as a research tool; inspiring new practices; building relationships and knowledge exchange (Lean 2020). I used these criteria to identify where textile thinking as a practice contributed to both exploratory and applied research within community-based, educational and policy environments. A contextual review led to identification of existing textile thinking in practice by researchers and practitioners, enabled coherent reporting on my own practice and resulted in a methodology which supports the position of textile design as a research platform in other fields.

To test the application of the established characteristi᷄ ˙textile thinking in my own practice under real-world conditions I undertoon ᷄olicy placement with the UK government's telecoms organization, Building Di᷄ ᷄ UK (BDUK). This setting provided the context for knowledge exchange using textile thinking approaches, which were used to engage people in research activities. The aim was to learn about the experiences of living with a high-speed internet connection. The outcomes of the research are insights about the impact of gigabit-capable connectivity which were presented to stakeholders and will inform the development of future interventions for demand stimulation – to encourage the uptake of fibre internet connections. The results (collected insights and a model for data collection) show how textile thinking approaches can be used to develop

"Slow down, cuz. I see yo' goofy ass off them pills again," he scoffed shaking his head. I was looking at Deja to see if she heard me and was happy as hell that she didn't.

"On Stone, I'm high as hell and I'm finna get higher," I bragged pulling out my phone to shoot Murda a text letting him know it was time to handle his business.

I sent the text then scanned the club trying to see who I recognized before someone bumped me hard as hell from behind.

"Watch where the fuck you going!" I gruffed, turning around to see Bone, Reese, Von D and Binky.

"Aw shit, they got my boy Binky back out here!" I said checking him out. He was skinny as hell and had to walk with a cane.

"I'm back out ready to put that belt on the first mufucka that look crazy," he replied making all us laugh. He was still on the same shit. I knew he couldn't wait to catch a body.

"You got skinny as hell lil bro," Nutso said giving him a hug. He was the happiest to have Binky back out. I knew pretty soon they were going to be inseparable.

"Them bullets knock weight off for real," Binky joked.

"Aye bitch, get my lil brother the biggest bottle of Remy y'all got in this bitch," I told a thick ass bottle girl throwing a few hundreds in her face.

"Aye chill the fuck out, cuz!" Nutso snapped

"Cuz, have you and stop talking to me like I'm yo son. I'ma grown man and if I wanna act crazy in this bitch, then I'ma act crazy. If I decide to shoot this bitch up, I'ma shoot this bitch up. Straight like that nigga," I told Nut, tired of him talking to me. He didn't reply. He just walked off into the sea of clubgoers.

"Shake that ass bitch!" T Stone yelled to a super thick, yellow boned stripper while throwing twenties and fifties at her.

"GET YOU A STONE. WE DO IT BETTER!" I yelled over the music looking at all my brothers enjoying themselves. The vibe was epic.

"If shorty keep twerking like that, I'm not sure I'ma leave this club, let alone the city," T Stone laughed as the stripper threw her gigantic ass in his face. I saw Binky creeping off with a bad ass stripper. I knew he was on his way to pay to play. It seemed like we were back in 2009 again. All the Moes popping our shit. That was until I seen Tippu headed our way with some unwelcomed guests.

\*\*\*

B Dub sat in the back room of the trap getting some top from a bitch named Angel, who he'd just met at the Louis Vuitton store earlier that day.

"Hurry up, shorty. We supposed to be at the club," he told her as she deepthroated him.

After a while she lifted her head, "You the one who won't cum you actin like you off a Viagra or something," Angel joked holding his dick in her hand.

"Stand up," he told her before pulling her up and bending her over the bed. He didn't even bother pulling off her thong. He just pulled it to the side and rammed his dick in and out of her pussy. B Dub focused on punishing her good pussy until he heard a knock at the door.

"You told somebody you was over here?" He asked Angel pulling his dick out of her.

"No," she replied breathing heavy.

He took a moment to think. He knew that Nut was at the club and he also knew that none of their workers or customers would be knocking on the door without calling first.

"Who the fuck is that?" He asked himself more than Angel when the door crashed in. "Act like you live here and you here alone. Whatever they ask for tell them, its in the closet," he told Angel in a hurried whisper before running to hide in the closet.

Breezy and Murda searched the front room of the seemingly empty crib looking for anything of value to take.

"This bitch too quiet," Murda mumbled heading for the kitchen. He looked in every room along the way and stopped when one of the bedroom's door was closed. He opened the door waving his Glock 19 with a drum and a red beam to see a pretty, thick, caramel skinned woman standing in a mirror dressed in only her bra and panties. The room smelled like Kush smoke and sex.

"Where the work at bitch?" Murda yelled at the woman who looked like she was scared shitless.

"Please don't shoot!" Angel yelled with tears falling from her eyes.

"Bitch, where the money and drugs at?" He yelled staring at her perky breast.

"It's all in the closet," she whimpered pointing towards the closet.

Murda approached the closet carelessly which was a costly mistake because when he swung the closet's door open, he was greeted by the end of B Dub's SK. The first shot almost removed Murda' s head from his shoulders. Angel shrieked loudly as his body crumbled to the floor.

Breezy ran in the room to see Murda dropping and turned around to run but not without recklessly shooting his Glock behind his back. B Dub sent a few shots in Breezy's direction all while trying to prevent catching a bullet himself.

"Shorty come on. We gotta slide," B Dub told Angel not even chasing Breezy.

"Okay, let me get dressed," she told him searching for her clothes.

"Bitch ass nigga," B Dub said looking at Murda one more time before shooting Angel in her chest with the SK. He was going to let her live but he thought about the fact that he had just murdered someone in front of her and he barely knew her so she had to go. "Can't leave no witnesses baby," he told her as he watched her choking on her on blood.

***

"Aye look Moe," I told T Stone nodding in the direction that Tippu was coming from. He was followed by Reesie, Cello, Racks and a gang of other niggas. Some I knew, some I didn't know.

T Stone pushed the stripper from in front of him and stood up.

"Tippu, what you on?" He asked, mugging Reesie and his crowd.

"Shit, I just thought I should bring everybody to yo' going away party. On the Foe, I'm sure ain't nobody gon' forget this one," Tippu replied with a sinister smirk on his face. He was a Four Corner Hustler so I wasn't surprised to see him with Reesie nem.

"T Stone, you been rocking with these bitch ass niggas?" I asked keeping my eyes on Reesie. He had on a thick Cuban Link with a Double R pendant. The Double R's stood for Risky Road.

"Hell naw," T Stone replied honestly. Reesie had a look in his eyes that said that he was on bullshit as usual.

"Fuck is you looking at you bitch ass nigga?" I barked cocking my Gucci hat to the left.

"Yo bitch ass," Reesie replied without fear.

"How you wanna do it then?" I asked dropping my hand near my waistline.

"We got a lotta those," he replied, unmoved by my gesture.

Just as I was about to respond, French Montana's 'I Ain't Worried About Nothin' came on and the club went crazy.

"I AIN'T WORRIED BOUT NOTHIN!" I yelled with French Montana and started jumping around to the song. By now, Bone, Nutso and a lot of the Moes were ganged up behind me just as geeked as I was.

"Bitch ass niggas! Fuck the Foes!" I said dropping the Four Corner Hustler gang sign.

Reesie and his crowd followed suit and started dropping the five at me and the Moes. Somehow, some way, our crowds merged and a lot of bumping and shoving went on until somebody went upside my head with a Hennessy bottle. I tried to regain my composure as another attacker rained blows on my head. I felt more people punching on me so I knew that the club was going up. Us versus them. I looked up to see Binky go across the nigga who was punching me head with his cane. My attacker turned out to be the nigga Lil Jay, who I had robbed in Nutso's trap. I don't know what he was doing there or who he was with but he was the one who started the brawl. I saw Cello going toe to toe with T Stone and I snaked him knocking him on his ass. Before I could stomp him out, Reesie rushed me throwing punches. We went blow for blow. We traded love and hate with every punch we connected. Reesie connected a nasty two punch combo that split my lip before I kicked him in the bad leg that I shot him in. After both of us threw another flurry of punches, we were tired and had started wrestling.

"Yeaaaa!" Reesie said when he mounted me and wrapped his skinny fingers around my neck. I started to see black spots when Nutso saved the day by hitting Reesie with a bottle of Ace of Spades. As I got up, I peeped Bone, stomping Cello out. I headed that way to help and saw Lexi hit Bone in the back of the head with a bottle.

"I caught yo' sneaky ass, bitch!" I growled grabbing a handful of Lexi's hair as she tried to run off. I cocked my arm back to break her jaw, but somebody grabbed my wrist.

"Let her go," Nutso told me, squeezing my wrist.

"On Stone, she just snaked Bone," I said tightening my grip on her hair.

"Cello is her cousin. She supposed to help him. Now let her go," he said sternly.

I muffed Lexi hard making her stumble and fall to the floor.

Nutso pushed me and ran to assist his bitch.

'Bitch ass nigga' I thought as I upped my gun and shot in the air causing mayhem.

Outside the club was hectic. It was so many fights going on that the police couldn't stop them all.

"Dre come on!" Deja screamed standing next to my Charger that I had her rent.

"Give me the key to the rental and you drive my car," I told her.

"No, I'm not leaving without you," she replied stubbornly. I knew she was high off a half a pill and maybe drunk too so I didn't snap on her like I wanted to.

"Get down bae," I said as I seen Reesie heading our way trying to be discreet about it.

"What?" She asked before I took off running. Reesie chased me down dumping shot after shot as I ran through the club's parking lot. I saw Binky limping my way and I pushed him to the ground trying to get away from Reesie.

"Hop in Moe!" T Stone yelled in his Challenger. I ducked low and ran to the car hoping that I didn't get hit along the way.

"GO! GO! GO!" I told him when I jumped into his passenger's seat, and he peeled off.

Binky was mad as hell as he got up from the ground. Reesie could've killed him if he wasn't so hellbent on killing me. His legs were killing him and he needed to sit down. The parking lot was pure chaos. He heard multiple guns going off and the loud wail of police sirens. He saw me and T Stone riding by and tried to flag us down. We locked eyes but I told T Stone to keep going.

Binky pulled out his phone to call Bone or somebody until he felt a arm wrap around his shoulder. He looked over knowing it had to be one of the guys and was surprised to see Kevin Foe standing next to him with a devilish grin on his face.

"What's the word?" Binky said, knocking his arm off his shoulder.

"You know what it is," Kevin Foe said reaching for his gun but Binky was quicker. He shot him twice in the ribs. Kevin Foe stumbled but managed to up his gun and get a few shots off. Binky couldn't move like he wanted too so he caught a bullet to his shoulder,

'Damn I should have killed his goofy ass when I had the chance.' He thought just before Von D ran up and put Kevin Foe's brains on the pavement.

"Man, Mo Money bitch ass tried to get me smoked!" Binky yelled angrily.

"How?" Von asked helping him to his car.

"Reesie was chasing him and he threw me down knowing I can't run. Then, he hop in the car with T Stone and I tried to flag them down but they kept going on me!" Binky said seething with anger. Mo Money had just made his list. It was no way he was letting him get away with putting his life in jeopardy. If it wasn't for Von, he probably would've been dead because of Mo Money .

"Damn, law, I think I got hit," I told T Stone as we drove away from the club.

He pulled over on a dark side block and I bailed out the car and fell to the ground.

"You good bro?" T Stone asked rushing to check on me. When he turned me over, I shot him in his neck.

"I'm good now, you snake ass nigga," I said standing up watching him hold his bloody neck. I wanted him to suffer like I was suffering from losing my daughter but when I looked at him and only saw sadness mixed with confusion it hurt me. My feelings of anger ceased to exist. I was suddenly sorrowed for what I had to do.

"I'm sorry bro, I had to. Lopez said you gotta go in order for me to get Paradise back. I love you bro. I'm sorry," I told T Stone before putting two bullets in his head and running off.

I called Bone to come pick me up. I knew I couldn't walk back to the city with a murder weapon on me. Before Bone could make it to me, Nutso called me and told me some shit went down and to hurry up and meet him at my crib. He didn't tell me what happened so I feared the worst and prayed that everybody was okay. When we pulled up, I seen Deja balled up on the ground. Nutso, Lexi and a few other people were surrounding her.

"What happened to her?" I asked, rushing to her side. She was crying hard as hell and her jaw was red and puffy.

"I just knocked that bitch out!" Nutso gruffed, standing over us.

"Why?" I shouted, standing up ready to beat his ass.

"Because her brother tried to hit my spot!" Nutso yelled and spat in my face.

"Huh?" I asked looking crazy

"B Dub caught his bitch ass tryna hit the spot."

"So, where her brother at now?"

"B Dub clapped his hoe ass and then this bitch get to talking all crazy and shit so I knocked her ass out. Her weird ass probably the one who called the play,"

"She don't even know shit about yo' spot. She ain't call no fuckin play on you," I defended my bitch, helping her off the floor.

"They killed him," she cried burying her head in my chest. I really felt like shit because I was the reason he was dead.

"So, if she didn't put him on us, you the only other mufucka who could've told him anything about us," B Dub accused me.

"If it was me, we wouldn't be hitting the spot, we going to niggas' cribs where the real money at. Next time you insinuate me in some back door shit, I'ma take it there with you," I promised looking at him in his eyes.

"For real, though cuz," Nutso cut in.

"For real though what?" I asked screwing my face up.

"You and her the only ones with ties to her brother and if you so sure that she so innocent, then who was it blood?" Nutso asked dragging the blood.

"You tell me and you ain't been acting like blood lately. You can put that shit in yo' back pocket," I told him opening my front door. "And next time any one of you bitch ass niggas come close to crossing that line with me or my bitch, I'ma smoke you. Ain't gon' be no talkin' about shit!" I promised before going in the house to comfort Deja.

# Chapter 13
## The Fall of Mo Money

I sat in Lopez's house surrounded by him and a few Latin kings.

"I handled that T Stone problem," I told Lopez. His eyes scanned my face looking for any signs of deceit or remorse.

"How?" He asked.

"What the fuck you mean how? I shot him. That's how," I replied sharply.

"When, where and how did it happen?" He asked with a looked of amusement on

his face.

"A few days ago. I tricked him into going to a strip club in the burbs with me. A fight broke out and amongst the struggle, I jumped in the car with him. We rode for a few blocks and I lied to him and said that I got hit. He pulled over and I shot him," I explained.

"Where did you shoot him at?"

"Once in the neck and twice in the face. The neck shot was for him to suffer and die slow, like I'm suffering not having my daughter but I didn't want to take any chances of him surviving so I put two in his face," I said. Lopez wanted me to be hurt that I had to kill one of my friends and even though it did hurt like a mufucka, I didn't want to give him the satisfaction of seeing that.

"Bring him his daughter," Lopez told one of the Kings. Moments later, I was playing with Paradise. She was getting taller and gaining weight and her hair was getting longer than it already was. I missed her badly.

"Do you miss me Paradise?" I asked her as she sat in my lap feeding me apple slices.

"Si," she replied in her sweet voice.

"Si?" I repeated screwing my face up. "AYE LOPEZ!" I shouted startling Paradise.

"Yes?" Lopez asked entering the living room.

"Why the fuck you got my daughter speaking Spanish and shit?" I asked sitting her down on his white Italian leather couch so I could stand face to face with him. I was mad as hell.

"Being bilingual is a very good thing. It's actually an advantage and will open many doors for her in the future," he explained with a smirk.

"On Stone, fuck all that shit. She a baby. The only language she needs to know is English," I snapped.

Lopez turned to Paradise. "Paradise you're looking pretty today," he told her.

"Gracias," she giggled.

My jaw dropped as I watched him chuckle.

"I don't find that shit funny. What if I took yo' daughter and taught her how to shoot dice and shake up Stone?" I asked picking Paradise up. "I got damn near a million of your dollars. I'ma be to get her real soon, my nigga. Until then, could you excuse us while we catch up," I said angrily.

After I left Lopez's home, I picked up Deja to take her on a date. I felt sorry for getting her brother killed, even though she didn't know I had anything to do with it. I wanted to make her feel better by dedicating a day to her. I knew she loved seafood, so we went to Two Fish, one of her favorite restaurants.

"Did I tell you how sexy you looking?" I said, as I admired the red shoulder less dress she wore. It clung to every curve her body had to offer.

"Thank you," she replied smiling from ear to ear as we entered the restaurant.

"Table for two," I told the guy at the front desk, not checking my surroundings.

"Bae, let's just go somewhere else," Deja said, grabbing my arm.

"Hell naw. Why? What's up?" I asked, taking off my White Sox fitted.

"There go Lil 4," she whispered, nodding in his direction.

"So. I got my pipe. He better have his if he play with me. I told you that tonight is all about you, baby. I'm not on none of that extra shit. I'm not gon' let nobody fuck up our night," I promised as the waiter led us to a table right next to Lil 4's. "What you 'bout to order?" I asked Deja completely ignoring Lil 4.

"I want some King Crab Legs. What about you?"

"I want some fish and shit," I replied making her burst out laughing.

"What kind of fish, retard?"

"Um I don't know. What's that fish you be making with the lemon pepper?" I asked, scratching my head.

"Tilapia. Tell them you want some baked Tilapia," she told me, smiling.

We made small talk while we waited for our food. Our vibe was fresh still and we still found each other extremely interesting. I loved her wit and sense of humor. She was almost as funny as I was.

"Girl, all this fish I'm smelling in the air got me thinking about what we did last night," I joked making her laugh.

"And what's that?" She asked knowing I was setting her up for a joke.

"When you was riding my face," I said, and we shared a good laugh. Today I hadn't gotten off the pill but I had been smoking so I was able to eat. I had almost forgotten how good food was. You can't eat off X pills so I was stuffing myself in preparation to pop after dinner.

"So, you telling me you never been to Six Flags?" I asked.

"No, but I always wanted to go,"

"I got you, but you better not be scared to get on the rides."

"So, were you in love with Precious ?"She asked after taking a sip of her Pepsi.

"Naw, not at first. I was just fucking her and she caught feelings. Then, when she got pregnant, I tried to get her to get an abortion. I wasn't ready for a child but she wasn't going. She thought if she had my child, she would win me but it didn't work like that. I ended up realizing how much I did love and respect her. She was a good person until she started tweaking. She always wanted to come first."

"Come first before who?" Deja asked.

I bit into a fried shrimp before answering, "She wanted to come before my first love, Ashley but in reality, Ashley didn't even come first."

"So, who came first?"

"The Trenches," I stated, thinking back. "I put the trenches before everything. I was young, wild and lit. I was in love with the streets and she did me wrong like every other bitch," I said gazing at my half eaten plate of food.

"How?"

"Because I got shot a million times. I lost a million friends. I lost my daughter. I'm losing myself and I lost Ashley," I said but caught myself. I didn't mean to say Ashley but she was on my mind.

"So, what's you and Ashley story?" Deja asked looking like she was truly interested and enjoying hearing about my life. I never spoke to her about Ashley. "She was my first love. We been through a lot together. She held me down through some of my best and worst times but,"

"But what?"

"But I guess she got tired of coming second to the streets. Before I got locked up, I had promised her that I was going to pay my plug the lil bread I owed him, leave the streets alone and settle down with her."

"And what happened?"

"After I paid the plug, I was still getting a lot of money. So much that I didn't want to stop anymore. Plus, I was obsessed with killing all the Foes. I was stuck in the streets. She found a boyfriend and I was fuckin hoes so we stopped communicating. Basically, I couldn't keep my promise," I admitted before noticing that Lil 4 was staring at me.

"What's up bro?" I asked, nodding at him with a smirk." I'm on a date bro. I'm not on that tonight. I don't want no smoke," I told him.

"Yup," He nodded pulling out his phone and texting somebody.

"Just because I'm not on that don't mean I won't fuck somebody up," I threatened patting the Glock on my waist.

"Let's just leave, baby," Deja whispered.

"No," I said shaking my head." This our night. I'm not letting nobody ruin our vibe so stop saying let's leave. I'm not going nowhere until I'm ready," I told her calmly. We conversed for a few more minutes until I was actually ready to slide.

"Aight, Lil 4, Be safe out here. I heard Moe nem was out riding," I joked as we walked past him and his BM.

When we got outside the restaurant I noticed a black Jeep creeping through the parking lot with no lights on.

"Fuck," I thought to myself, tightening my grip on Deja's hand. I braced myself as the Jeep slid up and the back window dropped. I shoved Deja to the ground so she wouldn't get hit by the bullets that I was sure were on their way.

"Bitch ass nigga," Reesie spat before rolling up his window. I looked and saw a blue and white police car riding through the lot too.

"I'm sorry bae. You straight?" I asked helping Deja off the ground.

"Yes, can we go home now?" She asked somberly with sadness dominating her expression. As we climbed into my car, my mother's words replayed in my head.

"Whatever you're doing out there son you need to stop it because you're going to end up getting yourself and everyone around you killed."

Every day that went past, her words haunted me and made me question whether I was really the bad guy.

"I'm sorry, bae," I told Deja as we rode off.

For the next few days, I stayed in the crib with Deja. I was back to my regular schedule, popping X pills like they were going out of style.

"Hello?" I answered my phone for Nut.

"What you on, cuz?" he asked.

"Shit in the crib with my bitch. What's the demo?"

"I need for you to make this run for me," he told me shocking me. Lately, he had been acting like he didn't trust me enough for me to make any runs for him.

"Yeah, you trust me enough now?" I asked sarcastically.

"Yeah, but my homie JB gone ride with you," he told me causing me to cut him off with laughter.

"There goes that trust," I said.

"Naw, these JB people that you going to serve. That's why he riding with you,"

"All well. When and where?"

"Right now and y'all ain't going nowhere far. Just Peoria," Nut said and hung up. I was hoping that whoever I was serving wanted more than one key cause I was about six hundred thousand dollars short of Lopez's money so it was crunch time.

I picked JB up off Interstate 290.

"What's good foe?" He asked getting into the passenger's seat of the rented Ford Mustang I was in. He was a light skinned nigga with a little acne and deep waves.

"I ain't no mufuckin' foe but what's the word?" I asked with a slight attitude.

JB didn't respond to me he just turned up the music and texted someone while we rode in silence. After a while, I started asking him questions just trying to pick his brain. I knew that nine times outta ten he wouldn't be making it back. I pulled into a Sonic's parking lot in a rest spot. "Let me see yo' phone," I told JB, cutting the car off.

"Why?"

"Text whoever we 'bout to serve and tell them to meet us right here," I said liking the location we were in. We weren't too far from the city so I could rob whoever was meeting us, hop back on the E way and be in the city in no time.

"That wasn't the plan," JB said.

"Man, do what the fuck I'm telling you to do!" I gruffed, quickly upping my .45

"Fuck is wrong with you dude?" JB asked. He wasn't showing any signs of fear.

"I'm 'bout to rob these bitch ass niggas," I confessed. I figured I could tell him since I planned on killing him anyway.

"You for real?" He asked with a smirk on his face.

"Do I gotta show you how for real I am?" I asked pressing the barrel against his temple.

"On the foe its crazy because I was 'bout to rob all y'all ass! "JB confessed shocking the hell outta me. I knew something was off about him.

"You dirty dog!" I said making him laugh." So, you was tryna get everybody huh?"

"Hell yeah. These niggas we meeting ain't really my people. Nutso lied to you so you wouldn't mind me riding along to babysit you. I was gone rob them and blame it on you."

"That bitch ass nigga," I said thinking about Nut. His bitch ass had really been pressing my buttons as of lately. "Look, I could clap you right now or we could hit this lick together and keep it between us," I said, giving JB a moment, trying to decide if he could trust me or not.

"On the foe, you got me at gunpoint so I don't got no choice but to join forces with yo' snake ass."

"Fasho," I said sitting my gun on my lap. I hopped back on the road and traveled to the original meeting spot.

JB sent a text and told the nigga Moss, who was buying the work, that we were there. He pulled up moments later in a navy blue Audi truck. Me and JB hopped out the car at the same time. I approached Moss's window.

" Where that bread at?" I asked him. He was a chubby, dark skinned guy with dreads.

"Hop in," he told me. I nodded at JB and we both climbed in the backseat. The front seat was occupied by another dread head." Let me check that work out." Moss said over his shoulder. He was answered by JB mashing his 9mm in his neck.

"You know what time it is," JB said through clinched jaws. Moss stomped the gas and then brake making the car jerk before speeding off. I heard JB's gun go off and that's when I jumped out the car and ran to my car jumping in. I was about to leave JB's goofy ass for fucking up the lick.

Before I could pull off, I saw JB jump out of Moss's truck and roll across the pavement.

"What happened?" I asked after driving to where he was and letting him in the car.

"When that hoe ass nigga pulled off, I shot his homie in his shit. I don't know what kind of Jackboy they thought I was. I do this shit for real," JB said. The hood that he was from out west called themselves the Jackboys.

"Man, you shoulda killed his hoe ass too. You know he bout to tell Nutso. I'ma just act like we never made it to serve him and that was somebody else who tried to rob him," I said already panicking. I knew once Nut found out I was doing this backdoor shit, he would automatically pin everything else that had happened on me.

"Right, so how we gon' handle that shit?"

I flamed up a wood before answering," Man fuck Nut. He ain't nobody. If anything, I'ma say dude tried to rob us and it's up to him who he believe," I said. I thought about killing JB for fucking up but I decided that since Murda was gone, I needed somebody else to hit licks with when I couldn't put my face on it.

I pulled out my phone to call Nut but he didn't answer.

Later that day I got a call from Nutso, a call that I knew was inevitable.

"What's the demo?" I answered dryly.

"On Stone cuz. All this time I been wondering why all my fucking clientele ain't been calling me back or why they all been coming up dead and it been you the whole time!" He yelled angrily.

"What the fuck is you talking about, cuz? "I asked feigning innocence.

"Moss called me and told me the hoe ass shit you and JB tried to pull. We out here making moves to help you get yo' daughter back and you doing all this  snake ass shit fuckin up business."

"Why you always throwing the fact that MY daughter gone in my face?" I asked, getting mad.

"Because I don't have no kids. I could be using my money for some whole other shit but I'm not. I'm giving it to you so you won't be miserable going through it. I'm out here putting in more effort than you."

"Nigga, fuck you!" I snapped. "On Stone, nigga I would smoke you and whoever riding with you. I'm tired of you, Lopez and everybody else that's in my way. I'm telling you cuz. I'ma start making examples outta you niggas," I yelled. " Nigga you ain't doing shit special. You doing what you supposed to do for family. This the type of shit that a make me get on some Bishop shit."

"Say less cuz. I'm cutting yo' water off. I bet you don't sell another drug in this city. You ain't gon' make another dollar if it's up to me."

"Please, cuz. You not El Chapo. Get yo' goofy ass outta here," I said blowing out a lungful of air. "Matter fact, like I said nigga. Fuck you. You better sleep on top of that money because that shit gon' get took," I said with ice in my tone before hanging up on him. I was so mad and frustrated that I couldn't help but let out a animalistic like roar. It seemed like shit just never worked out for me in life. I needed a plan.

The next morning, I decided to go somewhere I hadn't been since I was a young boy. Church. The Saint Matthews House of Praise was packed with God fearing people. Me with my designer clothes, rough looking dreads and not to mention I reeked of Kush smoke, I felt out of place. It seemed like all eyes were on me like the people in the church knew I needed a blessing or two. Me and Deja sat in the middle of the church as the choir sung a Marvin Sapp song. I hadn't been to church in over fifteen years, and it felt weird as the pastor preached his heart out. Not long after he started preaching, did they start passing out bread and wine. That's what they called it. I thought it was crackers and juice, but I didn't say shit.

"Fish and bread keep the poor man fed," I joked before drinking the wine. The pastor was speaking words that seemed to hit my heart like a bullseye. He kept mentioning betrayal, lies and death and I felt like he was directing that shit right at me. Every word hit head on. When the collection plate came around, I got a few stares due to the fact that I put a large wad of bills in it without even counting the money. The pastor, whose name was Pastor Ellis, words were so captivating that they had me in a trance. When he was done with his sermon, we locked eyes, and something told me don't leave.

"Come on bae," Deja said after she stood up, stretched and I didn't budge at all. I remained seated until we were the last two people in the pews. "What's wrong with you?" she asked as I stared at a sculpture of Jesus hanging from a cross.

"How are you doing today, young man?" Pastor Ellis asked me. His voice boomed throughout the empty room of the colorful church. He looked to be no older than thirty. He was a light brown complexion with a small curly fro.

"I'm straight. That was some nice shit that you was talking 'bout up there."

"That's not the choice of language that I would use in the house of the Lord but thank you," he told me with a stern look on his face.

"I felt like yo' whole sermon was dedicated to me. It's like you was speaking on everything that's going on in my life right now."

"And what's that?" Pastor Ellis asked and his question made me shoot him a funny look but the sincerity in his eyes was enough to make me let my guards down.

"Where should I start?" I asked myself after taking a deep breath. "First off, death been all around me and I know he waiting on me. He done touched me so many times but it's like he toying with me and tryna make me suffer, you feel me?" I asked and he nodded. "Then, betrayal been a constant theme in my life. I feel like everybody turned they back on me in one way or another and to be honest, I haven't been loyal either. Not to my friends or myself. I feel like I'm falling apart," I confessed.

"Have you ever heard of God breaking a man down all the way down just to rebuild him into a greater man?"

"I feel like he breaking me down to the point where he won't be able to rebuild me even if he wanted to."

Pastor Ellis nodded and handed me the bible he was holding. "Read Philippians, Chapter 4 verse 13," he told me.

"I can do all things through Christ who strengthens me," I read aloud.

"Right. Sometimes the Lord makes you feel weak only to show you how much strength you actually have."

"And how the fuck am I supposed to believe that?" I asked Paster Ellis, who shot me another stern look.

"You have to have faith. You have to believe and have hope."

"No disrespect but believing and having hope ain't never got me nowhere."

"What is it that you believe in? The streets? Money? Maybe you're having hope in the wrong things. Maybe your focused on things that you can't take with you on the day of judgement. If you ask me, I would tell you to give those things up and focus on family, peace and prosperity," he said placing a comforting hand on my shoulder. He spoke with confidence like he knew what he was talking about." I'll walk your lady friend to the door and while we walk and talk, I want you to get down on your knees, bow your head and pray. Don't get up until you've told the Lord everything you want him to know," he said before grabbing Deja's hand and leading her away from me. He must've known it would've been awkward for me praying in front of her and himself.

I walked to the front of the church where the sculpture of Jesus was and got down on my knees. I bowed my head, closed my eyes and placed my hands together. "Dear God, this yo' shorty Mo Money. I know I haven't been in tune with you in a long time but I'm going through it right now and I need you, gang. First off, please help me get my daughter back. I know it's really too late for me to be wishing I was a better father but she all I got and I'm all she got. Please help me get her back and I'ma do better. I'ma cherish every moment I get with her. I wanna apologize for all the bodies I caught and all the other sins I committed while doing me. Tell T Stone that I'm truly sorry but I had to do what I did. God if you hear me and you fucking with me, please try to understand what I'm really tryna say. Please help me turn my life around, not just for my daughter but for my OG and Deja too. I know I hurt a lotta people and I never once took the time to ask for forgiveness but I'm sorry God and if you give me another chance with my daughter, I'ma do my best as a father. Before I get up outta here Lord, tell Precious that I love and miss her and I won't never forget or replace her. Thanks God. I got a few more niggas to clap so I'm asking for forgiveness early. Well, that's all I'ma ask you for right now. Until next time, big bro. Amen," I said before lifting my head to see Pastor Ellis who was standing to my left with a smile on his face.

"Why the fuck was you eavesdropping on my prayers?" I growled upping my gun.

"Forgiveness comes to those who ask. Be blessed and start having faith. It's always sunshine after the rain," Pastor Ellis told me acting like he didn't even see the gun I had aimed at him." Let the Lord carry you, brother. Go ahead don't keep your lady friend waiting," he told me after handing me a gold rosary.

I stared at him in his long, burgundy robe. A strong aura radiated off of him and I felt nothing but goodness in his presence? "Thank you," I told him putting my gun on my waist and the rosary around my neck.

"Take the bible too and next time you decide to pay me a visit leave the gun at home or at least in the car," he told me and handed me the bible he was holding. I gave him a half hug and told him thanks one last time before leaving the church.

\*\*\*

"So, what's the word with yo' cousin? How we gon' carry him?" B Dub asked Nutso while keeping his eyes glued to the TV. He was playing an NBA game.

"Fuck that nigga. He was on some backdoor shit so he on his own," Nut replied. He was sitting on the couch with Lexi laying across his lap while he busted B Dub's ass.

"What about his daughter?" B Dub questioned making him think about his baby cousin.

"It ain't never fuck her but cuz made his bed so now he gotta lay in it."

"Basically, you saying fuck that pretty ass little girl. You wrong for that," Lexi said lifting her upper body from his lap.

"How am I wrong when it's her daddy that's fucking up?"

"Because it's clear that that boy is losing his mind behind what he's going through. Just imagine if someone were to kidnap your mother. How would you feel?"

"I would rob, steal and kill to get her back."

"Right, so how could you fault him for robbing, stealing and killing to get his first and only child back?" Lexi said, making it make sense.

Nutso didn't respond off back. He let her words soak in as he continued to play the game.

"Fuck that," he finally said. "If he a steal from us once, then he will do it every chance he get. Blood or no blood, I will smoke that nigga before I let him just take from me."

"A desperate man will do the unthinkable because he feel like he ain't got shit to lose," B Dub said.

"What that supposed to mean?" Nut asked, scratching his dreads.

"It ain't no telling what a nigga will do when his back against the wall, especially a nigga in Mo Money's situation."

"So, what you tryna say?"

"Didn't he tell you he will kill you and whoever else got in his way?"

"Yea and?"

"Think about it. By us cutting him off from making money, he might be looking at it like we're in his way."

It took a few seconds for what B Dub was saying to register in Nut's head.

"On Stone, he wouldn't kill me. His goofy ass was just talking," Nut stated firmly.

"I bet you thought he wouldn't steal from you either, right?"

"On Stone, cuz only doing that shit because the pills mixed with him stressing. That's not how he really coming," Nutso said, feeling himself getting frustrated.

"Well, you keep on believing that. Just remember that he yo' cousin not mine so if he come at me on some weird shit, I'ma clap his dumb ass," B Dub stated taking his eyes off the TV to look at Nutso.

"You ain't gon' kill my cousin and he not gon' come at you. Just chill and let me handle this," Nutso told B Dub but even he was unsure how things would play out.

# Chapter 14
## King Python

I had my face stuffed in Deja's pussy when my phone rang. It was a facetime call from Bone. I ignored the call and kept sucking on Deja's clit while she moaned and grinded her hips, pushing her pussy deeper into my face. Her legs trembled and she came on my lips as my phone rang again.

"What's good lil bro?" I asked with a slight hint of irritation in my tone.

"I got a power move for you to buss but you can't rob them," Bone told me.

"Who it is? What they want?" I asked, laying on my back while Deja got on top of me.

"It's a mufucka that's tryna buy a few keys from me and they overpaying like a mufucka," he replied excitedly.

"Who?" I asked as Deja bounced up and down on my dick.

"My big cousins, Meechie and Peezy. They up here visiting the family but they tryna take some shit back to Green Bay."

I contemplated while Deja continued to ride me. I was trying my best not to let a moan escape my mouth. "Bro that sound like the same shit that Killa was saying when he tried to *oop* me and Moe nem. I'm straight," I told Bone.

"Nigga, this family."

"Well, come get the keys and you serve them yo'self but I only got like six."

"They only want four."

"How much they paying?" I asked as I watched Deja rub her clit while she gyrated on my dick.

"I told them since they was family they can give me 180,000 dollars," Bone replied and I instantly nutted in Deja. I don't know if it was her good pussy or the amount of money he said but as soon as I heard the number, I exploded. Deja leaned forward to kiss me while my semihard dick was still inside of her. "Hello?" I heard Bone yell.

"Yeah bro. Come get the work and if they play with my bread, you might as well go back to Green Bay with they ass cause I'ma smoke you," I threatened and hung up the phone.

"Go get the shower ready for round two," I told Deja as I grinned, knowing that I was getting closer and closer to getting my daughter back.

After Bone successfully served his cousins, me and Deja counted out 1.1 million dollars. I had one key left and after that I was dry.

"Fuck, bae. After this last key what the fuck I'ma do?" I asked her. She was the only person that hadn't turned on me so far.

"Swallow your pride. Go talk to Nutso and let him know that you're sorry for your mistakes and that you still need his help."

I sighed deeply and shot her a funny look. "Fuck Nut. He made it clear that he didn't give a fuck about me or my daughter. I'm not 'bout to kiss his ass," I snapped.

"Stop being so stubborn and think about Paradise. Nut's your cousin go talk to him," she urged me. I looked into her beautiful eyes and my greatest idea popped into my head.

"Baby, you smarter than you look!" I told her before erupting in laughter. "Ima go pay Nut pussy ass a visit and when I leave, I guarantee that I'ma have enough bread to get Paradise back."

"You think he just gon' give you four hundred thousand?"

"No, dumb ass. I'm about to go take whatever lil money he sitting on at the crib," I told her, smiling from ear to ear.

"No, Dre please don't rob him. Just ask him for the money."

"I'm done asking for shit. I got my mind made up. I'm takin his bitch ass down tonight!" I said raising my voice in excitement before pulling out my phone.

An hour and a half later, me, Bone, Breezy and JB were all dressed in dark clothing waiting for Arab to pull up.

"Do Not shoot Nut," I told everybody for the hundredth time since we planned the robbery. "Take everything. Don't leave them niggas a penny or a gram!" I said as Deja let Arab into our home.

"I see you niggas thirsty on point. Who we taking down?" Arab asked shaking

up with me then Bone.

"Nut," I replied.

"Which Nut?"

"Nut, Nut. My mufuckin cousin. That nigga been tweaking, on Stone," I said trying to sound convincing.

"On Stone Moe, I'm a lot of things but I'm not a snake or a fake ass nigga so if y'all really bout to rob Nutso, then I'ma pass on that shit cause I fuck with him just like I fuck with you. If the shoe was on the other foot, I would be telling him the same thing," Arab told me.

As mad as I was, I couldn't blame him. I actually respected him for showing his loyalty.

"I guess I'ma just have to call yo' phone and tell you about it," I said with a small smirk.

"I don't even wanna hear about it bro," he replied before leaving the home.

"Anybody else scared?" I asked looking around the room. Once nobody replied, I grabbed my thirty shot Mac, chambered a round and led the way out the crib.

When we pulled up to Nutso's house, I noticed it was a few unfamiliar cars parked in front of his crib.

"Anybody in this bitch act crazy, pop his ass and ask questions later," I told them.

"Even Nut?" Bone asked chambering a bullet in his AK 47.

"Shoot Nut and I'ma leave yo' ass here," I promised getting out the car.

I knocked on Nut's front door and one of the guys named Boothie opened the door.

"Wassup, Moe?" Boothie asked nervously. Nut had given him and everybody else the word that I was on bone and that they weren't to fuck with me at all. Boothie regretted not looking through the peephole before opening the door especially when he saw Bone, Breezy and JB come from each side of the doorway with Choppas aimed at his face.

"Don't make a sound. Where everybody at?" I asked, entering the house with my eyes darting every direction.

"Everybody in the basement shooting dice," he stammered as I grabbed him and jabbed my Mac in his neck.

"You know the way," I told him pushing him towards the basement.

"Aye wait," Boothie said abruptly stopping mid step.

"What?" I gruffed extremely close to putting bullet in his ass.

"I know I fucked up by letting you in, bro. I know Nut gon' smoke me so let me just dip now, Moe. Fuck them other niggas," he pleaded.

"Give me yo' phone and dip," I told him taking his phone just in case he thought about getting smart and calling Nut to warn him. A big surge of adrenaline rushed through my body as I kicked in the basement door.

"First one of you bitch ass niggas move, gon' get smoked!" I barked, waving my Mac around the room. There had to be at least twenty men and women in the basement. Everybody was confused because they all knew me as Nut's cousin. I saw an older guy's hand drop near his waist and I put two bullets in his chest. That's when everybody knew it was real. "Anybody else wanna play stupid?" I asked.

Bone, Breezy and JB stood there silent with their Choppas aimed. The shit looked like a scene out of a movie.

"Cuz, what the fuck is you doing?" Nutso asked me. I could see the anger in his eyes.

"I'm robbing you. Fuck it look like I'm doing?" I asked with a sinister smirk on my face. "Bone, grab all that money off they ass and take any pipe you find," I instructed.

"You tweaking gang," B Dub told me with a mug on his face. I saw payback all in his eyes.

"Don't get fucked up, bro. I advise you to just shut the fuck up," I warned before turning my attention to Nut. "Where all the money and drugs at?" I asked him.

"I don't shit where I sleep," he stated.

"Come here, Lexi," I demanded, and she just looked at me like I was crazy.

"Bitch, don't make me come get you," I warned. When she got close enough, I grabbed her by her hair and shoved my Mac in her face.

"Cuz, if you love this bitch, then stop playing with me." Nutso shot me a smile. "Bro, keep her out of this shit."

"On Stone, I'ma kill this hoe in a few seconds if you don't give that shit up."

"Upstairs in my room. It's an electronic safe in the closet. The code is 00107," Nutso said defeatedly. I nodded at Bone, and he went upstairs to clear the safe.

"You ain't gotta do this shit, cuz. I was gon' put you back in the mix. I just had to sit you on the bench for a minute because you was getting too loose, but this ain't the way to go about it," Nut told me.

"I don't wanna hear that soft ass shit. Nigga, you was gon' let them Mexican mufuckas kill my daughter. Fuck you," I told him. "STOP MOVING!" I yelled to a squirming Lexi.

"You ready Law?" Bone asked returning with a small pillowcase halfway full of money. I frowned when I saw how small the pillowcase was.

"Man, cuz I see I'ma have to gon' head and kill this hoe to show you that I'm not playing," I said before slamming Lexi on the floor and pulling the trigger on the Mac. The whole room got eerily silent after the gunshot and Nut's jaw dropped. "Pick yo' lip up bitch. I ain't shot the hoe yet. You got one last chance to tell me where the money at or everybody in this bitch gon' die," I said looking at Lexi who was balled up on the floor, crying her eyes out.

"That's all that's in here," One of the Moes named Rich Homie said, and I popped him in his stomach.

"Didn't I say shut the fuck up?" I yelled hysterically.

"That shit in the air conditioner cuz," Nutso told me pointing towards a rusty old air conditioner that was sitting in the corner of the basement. Breezy went to the air conditioner and broke it open to see that it was stuffed with money.

"Thanks, cuz, I appreciate it," I said smiling like the cat who ate the canary as Bone and JB bagged up all the money.

"JB, you snake ass nigga," Nutso said spitting towards JB, making me laugh.

"Now, don't nobody move a muscle until I call Nut phone and say that y'all good. If anybody try to play Superman, he gon die. Matter fact, Nutso bring yo' goofy ass here," I told him. When he got close enough, I threw my arm around his shoulder. It was almost like I could feel the anger and hate radiating off of him. "You better hope these niggas love you enough not to act crazy," I mumbled to him.

JB played the back while Bone led the way to our car.

"This wasn't nothing personal, cuz, just business. You lucky I ain't take no drugs. I just need the money to get my baby back," I told him right before gunshots went off. I pushed him and ducked for cover as shot after shot rang out. I saw JB drop his Choppa and fall to the ground as I unloaded on the shooter who was Boothie snake ass. I saw Bone aim his Choppa at Nut but I jumped between them before he could let off a shot and get himself killed.

"WE GONE!" I yelled scrambling for our car. We jumped in and I pulled off. I saw JB chasing after the car, but this was his second time fucking up on a lick so I decided to keep going and let Nut deal with him.

On my way home, I texted Deja and told her to pack up everything we might need and be waiting for me in front of our crib. I wasn't about to sit there and wait for Nut or anybody else to come get us. I was about to tuck myself in a lowkey environment.

"I'm letting y'all know now that no matter how much money we got, I need five hundred thousand off back. Then, we gone split the rest," I told Bone and Breezy as we rode through the city streets.

"You can have all that shit, Moe. I know what it was for," Bone said from the passenger's seat. I peeped over and smiled at my lil brother. I admired that he had some stand up qualities.

"We should be decent with this lick here. I should be able to go get Paradise in the morning," I said as we pulled up in front of my crib. Deja was outside waiting.

"Meet me at the Congress Hotel downtown. Hurry up!" I told her throwing her my car key and the pillowcase full of money. I was sure that if Nut wasn't on his way here, then Lexi had most definitely dropped my Lo to Cello by now. Deja sensed my urgency and hurriedly put the bags in my car. I watched for a lil minute before pulling off.

Me and Bone drove in silence for a few minutes. My eyes darted back and forth from each of my mirrors looking for any sign of danger. My paranoia was kicking in.

"Damn man!" I gruffed.

"What's up?" Bone asked.

"My head all fucked up gang," I admitted.

"You will be all well in the morning once you get Paradise back. You did what you had to do for yo' shorty. That's what you was supposed to do. Anybody that's mad at you for that you gotta question them," Breezy said from the backseat.

I was about to respond but I was watching this black Infiniti truck that had been trailing us for a few blocks now. " This black Infiniti been behind us for a lil minute. Once we get to the light, we gone bail out and fuck that bitch up," I told them. We pulled to the light on 115th and Michigan and we all bounced out the car, shooting at the truck. The driver of the truck tried to reverse away from all the shooting but backed into a Buick. After emptying our clips in the window, we jumped back in the car and I peeled off the scene. I dropped Breezy off at his bitch crib and then me and Bone made our way to the Congress hotel to count out the money we hit for.

"You know if Nut come my way on some bullshit, I gotta do what I gotta do right?" Bone asked after a minute of riding silent.

"Do you," I replied before turning up the C-Money song that we were listening to. "You coming in?" I asked him as we pulled in front of the hotel.

"Yeah," Bone replied just as my phone rung.

"Hello?" I answered for the unknown number.

"They shot my baby up!" A woman's voice wailed through the phone.

"Who is this?"

"This Peaches. They done shot my baby up! I don't know if he's going to make it," my Auntie Peaches said sobbing.

"What happened?"

"I don't know. We're at Christ Hospital right now. He's in surgery," she cried.

"I'm on my way!" I said and hung up. "Nut just got shot up. They at Christ," I
told Bone before speeding off.

# Chapter 15
## Stuck On The Other Side

We rode in silence all the way to the hospital. I felt bad for doing what I just did and now my lil cousin could possibly be on his death bed. I didn't want our last memory of each other being me robbing him. Me and Bone entered the hospital looking suspect as hell. We were asking every doctor and nurse we passed about where we could find Nut at.

"Hey Dre!" I heard a vaguely familiar voice shout my name. I scanned the room and saw Ashley's mother, Mrs. Hassan waving me over with one hand and wiping tears off her face with the other.

"Hey, Mrs. Hassan. What's going on?" I asked.

"It's Ashley," she said before breaking down crying even harder than she already was. My heart rate doubled in pace.

"What's wrong with her?" I asked. She didn't respond. She just led me to where the patients were laying in their own respectable sections sectioned off by curtains. There Ashley was laying there. I almost started crying when I saw the condition she was in. It looked like she had been beaten damn near to death. Both of her lips were swollen and split open. One of her eyes were purple and swelled shut and the other was black too. From the crookedness of her nose, I assumed that it was broke.

"What the fuck happened to her?" I asked, balling my fist up. I was seeing red.

"She got into it with her boyfriend, and he hit her so she tried to stab him and he did this to her," Mrs. Hassan told me through the tears.

"Ashley, why didn't you call me?" I asked her, stroking her cheek with the back of my hand.

"She has a concussion, and the doctors said her ribs might be broken," Mrs. Hassan told me after Ashley was unresponsive.

"I promise. On everything I love I'ma kill that goofy ass nigga for doing this to her and I'ma be right here until she recover. I feel bad that I wasn't there to protect her so the least I could do is be her shoulder to lean on while she's healing."

"Thanks Dre, and as much as I hate a man who puts his hands on women, I don't want you to do anything to Dolla and get locked up for it. God don't like ugly so he'll get whatever he has coming."

I took another look at the love of my life and my mind was made up. Dolla was a dead man. He was my top priority.

"I'm sorry Mrs. Hassan but I wouldn't even lie to you and pretend that I'm letting something like this slide but my cousin got shot up. That's why I'm here. Let me go check on him and I'll be right back."

"Okay," she replied before I leaned over and kissed Ashley's swollen lips before taking off to see Nut.

When I entered Nut's hospital room, I immediately started thinking the worst. It looked like it was over with for cuz.

"Damn cuz, what happened?" I asked sadly.

"The doctors said they don't know if he'll make it or not. He still has a few bullets in him, and he needs to undergo one more surgery," Peaches told me, still crying. "He keep trying to talk. He's been asking for you," she told me squeezing his hand.

"Aight, let me holla at him alone. Bone in the waiting room. Go sit with him," I told her and she left. I came to

Nut's bedside to see that he had bloody patches all over his body and his skin was pale.

"I'm sorry, cuz," he whispered.

"You ain't got shit to be sorry about, cuz," I replied sitting next to his bed and grabbing his hand. Seeing him like this was too much for me and a tear slipped from my eye.

"I didn't try to do that shit," he replied.

"Who did this to you?" I asked.

"Cello and Reesie. Lexi called them after you left."

"I knew that bitch was on some snake shit. I'ma smoke that hoe!" I promised.

"I'm sorry, cuz. It was an accident," Nut apologized turning his head to look at me in my eyes.

"You sorry for what, cuz?"

Nutso coughed and more tears fell from my eyes. I was thinking that these were his last moments.

"I was trying to get Bone and I fucked up."

"What the fuck is you talking 'bout?" I asked, confused.

"I killed Precious," Nutso confessed and my grip on his hand tightened. I leaned closer putting my ear to his lips. "What?"

"I killed Precious cuz. I was supposed to been told you but I didn't know how," Nutso said.

I stood up and looked down at my cousin, who was also my best friend. My partner in crime. Me, him and Bone were Ed, Edd and Eddy. We had been inseparable since we were babies. I couldn't believe he was telling me that he was the one who killed my baby momma and could've killed my daughter. I took a deep breath before speaking.

"I love you, cuz. I'ma stand on Lexi, Reesie and Cello. Don't trip about that. You know how I'm coming for you. I just need for you to come from under this shit. You too strong to die now. It ain't yo' time," I said crying a little harder.

"Go get Paradise back and tell her I love her. I'm sorry cuz. I'm sorry," Nutso kept repeating.

"Stop talking. I love you," I told him before kissing him on his forehead.

I looked at the machine he was hooked up too and discreetly unplugged it before leaving the room.

"What did he say?" My auntie Peaches asked.

"Nothing much," I lied. "He sleeping, so let him rest for a lil minute. He gon' be okay, Auntie. I promise and you know I'm 'bout to go act crazy for him right now," I said with every intention of leaving the hospital and catching a body. I gave her a hug and a kiss on the cheek.

"Aye Bone, we gone," I told him heading for the exit.

I had on last thing on my agenda before I went home to count the money we came up on. I couldn't believe that I had just pulled the plug to end his life. I felt like I felt when I had to kill T Stone. I was sorry but I had to do it.

"Nut was the one who killed Precious," I told Bone as he drove up 95th Street. I couldn't think straight. I sat slumped in the passenger seat looking through the tinted window.

"How you know?" Bone asked.

"Because he just told me. He said he was tryna kill you," I told him as my phone vibrated. It was a text from Deja." Deja pregnant," I told Bone after reading the text. It was so much going on that I couldn't even be happy for real.

"Congratulations, Law," Bone said with a smile.

"They say every time you lose someone special, somebody else special is brough into your life. I lose Nut and find out I got a shorty on the way. Whoop-de-fuckin do," I said unenthusiastically.

"What you mean you lost Nut?" Bone asked looking over at me.

"I just pulled the plug on his bitch ass for killing Precious. Pull over though, I think I gotta throw up," I told Bone grabbing my stomach.

He pulled into an alley on 95th Street not too far from the Dan Ryan Expressway. I opened the door and climbed out. I bent over and started dry heaving. When I lifted up, I had my Mac in my hand.

"Nigga, I already knew what time it was. I saw it all in your eyes and heard it in yo' voice. You ain't good at disguising how you feel," Bone said with his Glock pointed at me.

"Bro, you almost got my daughter killed," I said with my finger on the trigger.

Bone smacked his lips. "It ain't even about that for real moe. It's about me and Precious, ain't it? You always thought you was the king and it hurt you that yo' queen chose the prince over you, right?" Bone asked with a smirk on his face.

"You ain't loyal gang," I replied.

"You ain't either."

BOOM. BOOM. BOOM. BOOM. BOOM. BOOM!

In jail, I learned that life was a game of chess. Chess was complicated and to be good at chess, you had to be strategic; sometimes you had to sacrifice your pawns, rooks, knights, bishops and even your queen just to make sure that the king is the last one standing. And above all else, you play to win the game. Always.

## To Be Continued...

# City of Smoke 3
# Coming Soon

# Lock Down Publications and Ca$h Presents
## Assisted Publishing Packages

| BASIC PACKAGE | UPGRADED PACKAGE |
|---|---|
| $499 | $800 |
| Editing | Typing |
| Cover Design | Editing |
| Formatting | Cover Design |
| | Formatting |
| **ADVANCE PACKAGE** | **LDP SUPREME PACKAGE** |
| $1,200 | $1,500 |
| Typing | Typing |
| Editing | Editing |
| Cover Design | Cover Design |
| Formatting | Formatting |
| Copyright registration | Copyright registration |
| Proofreading | Proofreading |
| Upload book to Amazon | Set up Amazon account |
| | Upload book to Amazon |
| | Advertise on LDP, Amazon and Facebook Page |

***Other services available upon request.
Additional charges may apply

**Lock Down Publications**
P.O. Box 944
Stockbridge, GA 30281-9998
Phone: 470 303-9761

# Submission Guideline

Submit the first three chapters of your completed manuscript to ldpsubmissions@gmail.com. In the subject line add **Your Book's Title**. The manuscript must be in a Word Doc file and sent as an attachment. Document should be in Times New Roman, double spaced, and in size 12 font. Also, provide your synopsis and full contact information. If sending multiple submissions, they must each be in a separate email.

Have a story but no way to send it electronically? You can still submit to LDP/Ca$h Presents. Send in the first three chapters, written or typed, of your completed manuscript to:

**LDP: Submissions Dept**
P.O. Box 944
Stockbridge, GA 30281-9998

*DO NOT send original manuscript. Must be a duplicate.* Provide your synopsis and a cover letter containing your full contact information.

Thanks for considering LDP and Ca$h Presents.

# NEW RELEASES

SANCTIFIED AND HORNY
by **XTASY**

THE PLUG OF LIL MEXICO 2
by **CHRIS GREEN**

THE BLACK DIAMOND CARTEL
by **SAYNOMORE**

THE BIRTH OF A GANGSTER 3
by **DELMONT PLAYER**

# Coming Soon from Lock Down Publications/Ca$h Presents

BLOOD OF A BOSS VI
SHADOWS OF THE GAME II
TRAP BASTARD II
By **Askari**

LOYAL TO THE GAME IV
By **T.J. & Jelissa**

TRUE SAVAGE VIII
MIDNIGHT CARTEL IV
DOPE BOY MAGIC IV
CITY OF KINGZ III
NIGHTMARE ON SILENT AVE II
THE PLUG OF LIL MEXICO II
CLASSIC CITY II
By **Chris Green**

BLAST FOR ME III
A SAVAGE DOPEBOY III
CUTTHROAT MAFIA III
DUFFLE BAG CARTEL VII
HEARTLESS GOON VI
By **Ghost**

A HUSTLER'S DECEIT III
KILL ZONE II
BAE BELONGS TO ME III
TIL DEATH II
By **Aryanna**

CITY OF SMOKE 2 | MOLOTTI

KING OF THE TRAP III
By **T.J. Edwards**

GORILLAZ IN THE BAY V
3X KRAZY III
STRAIGHT BEAST MODE III
By **De'Kari**

KINGPIN KILLAZ IV
STREET KINGS III
PAID IN BLOOD III
CARTEL KILLAZ IV
DOPE GODS III
By **Hood Rich**

SINS OF A HUSTLA II
By **ASAD**

YAYO V
BRED IN THE GAME 2
By **S. Allen**

THE STREETS WILL TALK II
By **Yolanda Moore**

SON OF A DOPE FIEND III
HEAVEN GOT A GHETTO III
SKI MASK MONEY III
By **Renta**

LOYALTY AIN'T PROMISED III
By **Keith Williams**

CITY OF SMOKE 2 | MOLOTTI

I'M NOTHING WITHOUT HIS LOVE II
SINS OF A THUG II
TO THE THUG I LOVED BEFORE II
IN A HUSTLER I TRUST II
By **Monet Dragun**

QUIET MONEY IV
EXTENDED CLIP III
THUG LIFE IV
By **Trai'Quan**

THE STREETS MADE ME IV
By **Larry D. Wright**

IF YOU CROSS ME ONCE III
ANGEL V
By **Anthony Fields**

THE STREETS WILL NEVER CLOSE IV
By **K'ajji**

HARD AND RUTHLESS III
KILLA KOUNTY IV
By **Khufu**

MONEY GAME III
By **Smoove Dolla**

MURDA WAS THE CASE III
**Elijah R. Freeman**

AN UNFORESEEN LOVE IV
BABY, I'M WINTERTIME COLD III
By **Meesha**

CITY OF SMOKE 2 | MOLOTTI

CITY OF SMOKE 2 | MOLOTTI

RAN OFF ON DA PLUG II
By **Paper Boi Rari**

HOOD CONSIGLIERE III
By **Keese**

PRETTY GIRLS DO NASTY THINGS II
By **Nicole Goosby**

PROTÉGÉ OF A LEGEND III
LOVE IN THE TRENCHES II
By **Corey Robinson**

IT'S JUST ME AND YOU II
By **Ah'Million**

FOREVER GANGSTA III
By **Adrian Dulan**

GORILLAZ IN THE TRENCHES II
By **SayNoMore**

THE COCAINE PRINCESS VIII
By **King Rio**

CRIME BOSS II
By **Playa Ray**

LOYALTY IS EVERYTHING III
By **Molotti**

HERE TODAY GONE TOMORROW II
By **Fly Rock**

CITY OF SMOKE 2 | MOLOTTI

REAL G'S MOVE IN SILENCE II
By **Von Diesel**

GRIMEY WAYS IV
By **Ray Vinci**

# Available Now

RESTRAINING ORDER I & II
By **CA$H & Coffee**

LOVE KNOWS NO BOUNDARIES I II & III
By **Coffee**

RAISED AS A GOON I, II, III & IV
BRED BY THE SLUMS I, II, III
BLAST FOR ME I & II
ROTTEN TO THE CORE I II III
A BRONX TALE I, II, III
DUFFLE BAG CARTEL I II III IV V VI
HEARTLESS GOON I II III IV V
A SAVAGE DOPEBOY I II
DRUG LORDS I II III
CUTTHROAT MAFIA I II
KING OF THE TRENCHES
By **Ghost**

LAY IT DOWN I & II
LAST OF A DYING BREED I II
BLOOD STAINS OF A SHOTTA I & II III
By **Jamaica**

LOYAL TO THE GAME I II III
LIFE OF SIN I, II III
By **TJ & Jelissa**

IF LOVING HIM IS WRONG…I & II
LOVE ME EVEN WHEN IT HURTS I II III
By **Jelissa**

CITY OF SMOKE 2 | MOLOTTI

BLOODY COMMAS I & II
SKI MASK CARTEL I, II & III
KING OF NEW YORK I II, III IV V
RISE TO POWER I II III
COKE KINGS I II III IV V
BORN HEARTLESS I II III IV
KING OF THE TRAP I II
By **T.J. Edwards**

WHEN THE STREETS CLAP BACK I & II III
THE HEART OF A SAVAGE I II III IV
MONEY MAFIA I II
LOYAL TO THE SOIL I II III
By **Jibril Williams**

A DISTINGUISHED THUG STOLE MY HEART I II &
III
LOVE SHOULDN'T HURT I II III IV
RENEGADE BOYS I II III IV
PAID IN KARMA I II III
SAVAGE STORMS I II III
AN UNFORESEEN LOVE I II III
BABY, I'M WINTERTIME COLD I II
By **Meesha**

A GANGSTER'S CODE I &, II III
A GANGSTER'S SYN I II III
THE SAVAGE LIFE I II III
CHAINED TO THE STREETS I II III
BLOOD ON THE MONEY I II III
A GANGSTA'S PAIN I II III
By **J-Blunt**

PUSH IT TO THE LIMIT
By **Bre' Hayes**

CITY OF SMOKE 2 | MOLOTTI


BLOOD OF A BOSS I, II, III, IV, V
SHADOWS OF THE GAME
TRAP BASTARD
By **Askari**

THE STREETS BLEED MURDER I, II & III
THE HEART OF A GANGSTA I II& III
By **Jerry Jackson**

CUM FOR ME I II III IV V VI VII VIII
An **LDP Erotica Collaboration**

BRIDE OF A HUSTLA I II & II
THE FETTI GIRLS I, II& III
CORRUPTED BY A GANGSTA I, II III, IV
BLINDED BY HIS LOVE
THE PRICE YOU PAY FOR LOVE I, II ,III
DOPE GIRL MAGIC I II III
By **Destiny Skai**

WHEN A GOOD GIRL GOES BAD
By **Adrienne**

A GANGSTER'S REVENGE I II III & IV
THE BOSS MAN'S DAUGHTERS I II III IV V
A SAVAGE LOVE  I & II
BAE BELONGS TO ME I II
A HUSTLER'S DECEIT I, II, III
WHAT BAD BITCHES DO I, II, III
SOUL OF A MONSTER I II III
KILL ZONE
A DOPE BOY'S QUEEN I II III
TIL DEATH
By **Aryanna**

CITY OF SMOKE 2 | MOLOTTI

THE COST OF LOYALTY I II III
**By Kweli**

A KINGPIN'S AMBITION
A KINGPIN'S AMBITION **II**
I MURDER FOR THE DOUGH
By **Ambitious**

TRUE SAVAGE I II III IV V VI VII
DOPE BOY MAGIC I, II, III
MIDNIGHT CARTEL I II III
CITY OF KINGZ I II
NIGHTMARE ON SILENT AVE
THE PLUG OF LIL MEXICO II
CLASSIC CITY
By **Chris Green**

A DOPEBOY'S PRAYER
By **Eddie "Wolf" Lee**

THE KING CARTEL I, II & III
By **Frank Gresham**

THESE NIGGAS AIN'T LOYAL I, II & III
By **Nikki Tee**

GANGSTA SHYT I II &III
By **CATO**

THE ULTIMATE BETRAYAL
By **Phoenix**

BOSS'N UP I, II & III
By **Royal Nicole**

CITY OF SMOKE 2 | MOLOTTI

I LOVE YOU TO DEATH
By **Destiny J**

I RIDE FOR MY HITTA
I STILL RIDE FOR MY HITTA
By **Misty Holt**

LOVE & CHASIN' PAPER
By **Qay Crockett**

TO DIE IN VAIN
SINS OF A HUSTLA
By **ASAD**

BROOKLYN HUSTLAZ
By **Boogsy Morina**

BROOKLYN ON LOCK I & II
By **Sonovia**

GANGSTA CITY
By **Teddy Duke**

A DRUG KING AND HIS DIAMOND I & II III
A DOPEMAN'S RICHES
HER MAN, MINE'S TOO I, II
CASH MONEY HO'S
THE WIFEY I USED TO BE I II
PRETTY GIRLS DO NASTY THINGS
**By Nicole Goosby**

LIPSTICK KILLAH I, II, III
CRIME OF PASSION I II & III
FRIEND OR FOE I II III
By **Mimi**

TRAPHOUSE KING I II & III
KINGPIN KILLAZ I II III
STREET KINGS I II
PAID IN BLOOD I II
CARTEL KILLAZ I II III
DOPE GODS I II
By **Hood Rich**

STEADY MOBBN' I, II, III
THE STREETS STAINED MY SOUL I II III
By **Marcellus Allen**

WHO SHOT YA I, II, III
SON OF A DOPE FIEND I II
HEAVEN GOT A GHETTO I II
SKI MASK MONEY I II
By **Renta**

GORILLAZ IN THE BAY I II III IV
TEARS OF A GANGSTA I II
3X KRAZY I II
STRAIGHT BEAST MODE I II
By **DE'KARI**

TRIGGADALE I II III
MURDA WAS THE CASE I II
By **Elijah R. Freeman**

THE STREETS ARE CALLING
By **Duquie Wilson**

SLAUGHTER GANG I II III
RUTHLESS HEART I II III
By **Willie Slaughter**

CITY OF SMOKE 2 | MOLOTTI

GOD BLESS THE TRAPPERS I, II, III
THESE SCANDALOUS STREETS I, II, III
FEAR MY GANGSTA I, II, III IV, V
THESE STREETS DON'T LOVE NOBODY I, II
BURY ME A G I, II, III, IV, V
A GANGSTA'S EMPIRE I, II, III, IV
THE DOPEMAN'S BODYGAURD I II
THE REALEST KILLAZ I II III
THE LAST OF THE OGS I II III
By **Tranay Adams**

MARRIED TO A BOSS I II III
By **Destiny Skai & Chris Green**

KINGZ OF THE GAME I II III IV V VI VII
CRIME BOSS
By **Playa Ray**

FUK SHYT
By **Blakk Diamond**

DON'T F#CK WITH MY HEART I II
By **Linnea**

ADDICTED TO THE DRAMA I II III
IN THE ARM OF HIS BOSS II
By **Jamila**

YAYO I II III IV
A SHOOTER'S AMBITION I II
BRED IN THE GAME
By **S. Allen**

LOYALTY AIN'T PROMISED I II
By **Keith Williams**

CITY OF SMOKE 2 | MOLOTTI

TRAP GOD  I II III
RICH $AVAGE I II III
MONEY IN THE GRAVE I II III
By **Martell Troublesome Bolden**

FOREVER GANGSTA I II
GLOCKS ON SATIN SHEETS I II
By **Adrian Dulan**

TOE TAGZ I II III IV
LEVELS TO THIS SHYT I II
IT'S JUST ME AND YOU
By **Ah'Million**

KINGPIN DREAMS I II III
RAN OFF ON DA PLUG
By **Paper Boi Rari**

CONFESSIONS OF A GANGSTA I II III IV
CONFESSIONS OF A JACKBOY I II
By **Nicholas Lock**

I'M NOTHING WITHOUT HIS LOVE
SINS OF A THUG
TO THE THUG I LOVED BEFORE
A GANGSTA SAVED XMAS
IN A HUSTLER I TRUST
By **Monet Dragun**

QUIET MONEY I II III
THUG LIFE I II III
EXTENDED CLIP I II
A GANGSTA'S PARADISE
By **Trai'Quan**

CITY OF SMOKE 2 | MOLOTTI

THE ULTIMATE SACRIFICE I, II, III, IV, V, VI
KHADIFI
IF YOU CROSS ME ONCE I II
ANGEL I II III IV
IN THE BLINK OF AN EYE
By **Anthony Fields**

THE LIFE OF A HOOD STAR
By **Ca$h & Rashia Wilson**

THE STREETS WILL NEVER CLOSE I II III
By **K'ajji**

NIGHTMARES OF A HUSTLA I II III
By **King Dream**

HARD AND RUTHLESS I II
MOB TOWN 251
THE BILLIONAIRE BENTLEYS I II III
REAL G'S MOVE IN SILENCE
By **Von Diesel**

GHOST MOB
By **Stilloan Robinson**

MOB TIES I II III IV V VI
SOUL OF A HUSTLER, HEART OF A KILLER I II
GORILLAZ IN THE TRENCHES
By **SayNoMore**

BODYMORE MURDERLAND I II III
THE BIRTH OF A GANGSTER I II
By **Delmont Player**

CITY OF SMOKE 2 | MOLOTTI

FOR THE LOVE OF A BOSS
By **C. D. Blue**

KILLA KOUNTY I II III IV
**By Khufu**

MOBBED UP I II III IV
THE BRICK MAN I II III IV V
THE COCAINE PRINCESS I II III IV V VI VII
By **King Rio**

MONEY GAME I II
By **Smoove Dolla**

A GANGSTA'S KARMA I II III
By **FLAME**

KING OF THE TRENCHES I II III
By **GHOST & TRANAY ADAMS**

QUEEN OF THE ZOO I II
By **Black Migo**

GRIMEY WAYS I II III
By **Ray Vinci**

XMAS WITH AN ATL SHOOTER
By **Ca$h & Destiny Skai**

KING KILLA
By **Vincent "Vitto" Holloway**

BETRAYAL OF A THUG I II
By **Fre$h**